SPENCER'S LAW

By

Michael T. Gmoser

Michael T. Gmoser

Spencer's Law
By Michael T. Gmoser
Cover by Jan Kostka
Wrong Way Books an imprint of
Winged Hussar Publishing,
LLC, 1525 Hulse Road, Unit 1, Point Pleasant, NJ 08742

This edition published in 2021 Copyright ©Winged Hussar Publishing, LLC

ISBN 978-1-950423-59-0
Library of Congress No. 2021938309
Bibliographical references and index
1. Legal procedural 2. Mystery 3. Action & Adventure

For more information on Winged Hussar Publishing, LLC, visit us at:
 https://www.WingedHussarPublishing.com
Twitter: WingHusPubLLC
Facebook: Winged Hussar Publishing LLC

FRIDAY

4:20 P.M.

Chapter One

As Alice Simpson left her ob-gyn's office, she was relieved that all was well with her first pregnancy. Dr. Thomas told her that she was on schedule for delivery in four weeks and that all tests, including her latest amniocentesis, were normal. His final physical examination was comprehensive – taking all her and the baby's vital signs, answering all her questions and explained where the baby was positioned. He made a small red mark with a felt-tipped pen, so she could show her husband where the baby's head was now, and again with the pen where he expected it to be in a month during the anticipated normal delivery. This was her last visit on her own. The doctor told her that after that from now on, driving was simply too dangerous and should be avoided, even though winter was nearly over as far as the calendar was concerned. Making her way to her car, she felt a little stuffy and chilled, but inside the car the bright Friday afternoon sun had warmed the seat and she looked forward to the weekend ahead and a relaxing drive from the city to the country where she lived with her husband, two cats, and a dog named Charlie.

She and her husband, Professor Carl Simpson, looked forward to starting a family with great anticipation. Professor Simpson was a brilliant physicist and was one of those child prodigies often heard about, but seldom seen. Up to now, his professional life centered on his bevy of graduate students at the university where he taught physics and did advanced research on the cosmos. His personal life was simply devotion to Alice who forgave him all his faults as the truly absent-minded professor that he was around their home. She did this because he explained, in the most romantic way, that her existence confirmed the mysteries of the universe he sought so hard to explain. She never could understand his true meaning, but she always knew it was profound from one who should know. That was enough for her. In the constellation of stars that swirled around in his head, she knew her place was in the center, and she accepted her role-to-be as a homemaker and mother. She was well read and educated and, while not the intellectual equal to Carl (no one was), she had artistic talent to complement Carl's reality-based world, and that appealed to him. Life was good for both, and now it could only get better. Her drive home took her over sparsely populated country roads with only an occasional farm house and open fields in view. She relaxed as the traffic went from complicated to almost nonexistent. This was always the part of a solitary drive on any occasion that she enjoyed the most. It was a time for reflection and even relaxation in spite of her condition. Spring was fast approaching, and there was a telltale light green cast to the budding trees that fulfilled the promise of the new season to come. "New life", she thought smiling, "was pushing through," and she would soon be a part of that great story in her own way.

She knew that when she arrived home Carl might already be there. He had planned to take her to see Dr. Thomas, but his schedule could not be changed, and Dr. Thomas assured them both on her prior visit that she could handle the trip alone. "He was right as usual," she concluded. She hoped Carl would be home because she knew he would ask if the doctor slipped up, disclosing the gender that she and Carl had decided to keep secret, even from themselves. Still, Carl's inherent curiosity was getting the best of him, and she would have to joyfully tell him that it was still a part of the great unknown when he pressed her for an answer.

Letting her mind wander on her family-life-to-be, she did not notice a car fast approaching in her rear view mirror. Moments before impact she saw the danger and felt helpless to avoid the crash that sent her into the ditch. She was now stuck in the ditch with the engine still running and her tires spinning uselessly. There was no fire. She felt no pain. She quickly shut off the ignition with the realization that driving out of the ditch was not an option and looked around. The car that hit her had left the scene. "What a jerk! What person does such a thing?" she thought, but there was no time for further

7

reflection. She was remarkably calm considering what just happened and sensed she was not seriously injured, but alone except for a farm tractor that was not far off and plowing away from her. The farmer seemed oblivious to anything around him while sitting in the cab of his gigantic, climate-controlled, and enclosed tractor, except for the path he was plowing ahead on his near mile-long electronic course. With his course set driven by a GPS-controlled autopilot, and with his stereo set on high, not even the sound of the crash could penetrate his office on wheels. Eventually, the farmer would have to turn and perhaps then he might see her and come to her aid. Only minutes before she had been comfortably alone on the country road having survived the crash. Now she felt a sense of desolation and dread.

Calling Carl was her best option, she thought. He needed to know that she was okay and would be late. Before doing that, she would have to find the phone that probably went flying with her purse when she hit the ditch. Her thoughts also quickly turned to her pregnancy, and the possibility of her water breaking. She learned this much in the preceding eight months about how her water may break unexpectedly during her pregnancy, and she was mentally prepared for such an emergency. As far as she could tell, that had not happened. Since the airbag had not deployed, she could at least get out of the car, if necessary, but assessed that it was far better to remain where she was inside the car. Besides, it was getting colder, and it made no sense to trade a warm place for a cold one. With careful twisting and leaning from the driver's side, she saw the contents of her purse on the floor behind her, but her phone was not there. She was able to reach her purse and what remained in it. Everything else was in view on the floor, she thought, but it did not include her cell phone. Searching for it might take some time, but Carl had installed a new and improved battery that could last for weeks, and it was fully charged. She spilled the remaining contents on the passenger seat, but the cell phone was not there. She felt certain she had it with her when she left the doctor's office. She used it several times while there to check her emails and it was always in her purse that she kept with her except when the nurse asked for two urine samples. Now it could be anywhere in her car and probably under the seat that she could not reach unless she would have to get out and work her way around the car. The depth of the ditch did not make that thought an appealing option but seemed to be a necessary one.

Just as she was reaching for the door handle, she heard the welcoming sound of a siren. "Someone somewhere must have called it in," she thought. She waited for whatever it was to pull up behind her and was confident that whoever it was would be able to contact Carl and let him know that all was well. She saw an ambulance slowing down and she could see a driver and at least one passenger in the front seat. The ambulance came to a stop. The passenger, wearing blue nitrile gloves and a turquoise medical mask, approached her. The driver, in the same gloves and mask remained with his hands on the wheel in the driver's seat. As the passenger walked up to Alice's car, he signaled her to roll down her window. Since the window wasn't working, she opened the door to explain her situation.

"Are you okay?" the man asked. He had a slight accent, but all she could see of his face were his dark almost black eyes and a thin visible scar running vertically from his hairline. His eyes and the scar were his only defining characteristics. "We are just coming back from an emergency and trying to maintain sterility. I mean, we wear these masks and gloves to avoid contamination for our patient. Sorry, if we look like Halloween characters," he said.

"I think I'm fine," she answered. "Somebody just ran me off the road, and I would really appreciate a call to my husband to let him know I'm all right. I can't find my phone."
"No problem. My phone is in the ambulance, and it looks like you are in a family way," he said with a compassionate tone. "You really ought to let us check you out to make sure. Don't worry. There's no charge, and as long as we're here, and we will be happy to do it while we make a call to your husband."

"Sounds like a plan," she said, as she pushed open her door further to assess her footing.

"You better let me help you out of your car. The ground here is really uneven, and you might fall. We don't want to turn a good deed into a bad one, if you get my meaning." He carefully assisted her out to a standing position.

"Wow, I feel dizzy now – from standing up. I suppose getting checked out is a good idea, after all. Do I need a mask, too?" she asked looking at his mask.

"In a minute, yes, but don't worry about it. It won't take long to check you out."

As they all arrived at the rear of the ambulance including the driver, the rear door was wide open and a gurney was out just in front of it. A third member of the ambulance squad, whom Alice hadn't seen earlier, was standing by the gurney. He was also wearing a mask and gloves and forcibly and unceremoniously pushed her on to the gurney. In what seemed only an instant, she felt her arms grasped and held in place, while her hands and legs were tied to the gurney.

"What are you doing?" Alice screamed in disbelief of what was happening. She repeated that simple question several times, until she realized that she was being totally ignored. Her screams meant nothing to the very men she had thought were her rescuers. She was being kidnapped, she realized, but she could not wrap her mind around why it was happening to her. The collapsible gurney was pushed and raised into the ambulance. There were now four squad members standing over her looking down, wearing masks and gloves, and in paramedic uniforms. Alice was able to tell from the voice of one that one was a woman, but with the masks, there was little else that she could tell about them except the one who first spoke to her with an accent, dark eyes and facial scar.

"Let's get on with it – 72 seconds," one said, and the other who met her first knelt down beside her. As all this was happening, Alice was paralyzed by fear, and she was not able to comprehend what was happening. She lived a sheltered life, and what was about to happen was beyond her experience. She only knew of trauma and terror from the evening news from events in faraway places. She was now in the middle of both as her clothing over her belly was cut away by the one at her side.

10

Michael T. Gmoser

"Stop! Please stop!" she pleaded and struggled against the ties on her wrists and feet. "What are you doing to me? Please, please stop!" she begged.

"Scalpel," the man beside her demanded, and was handed the surgical blade.

Alice saw the blade and began to scream uncontrollably, trying to break the bonds that held her arms and legs in an effort to get away. Now she not only understood that a kidnapping was in progress, but she also realized her baby was going to be cut out of her. She had a fleeting memory of a report in a Chicago newspaper about a woman and a baby in a similar attack. The woman was murdered in the surgical process and her baby did not survive the kidnapping. That happened in a back alley by amateurs, she recalled, and to her this seemed, at least, to be done by professionals.

"Shut her up."

"We should just kill her now and make it a lot easier," a male voice was heard to say as the same person stuffed a rag in her mouth. "88 seconds," he added.

"No. We can't risk the trauma to the baby. You know that, but I will kill that son-of-a-bitch, if it's not a boy. This should be easy. The baby is positioned perfectly for a lateral approach, and we should be outta here on schedule. Everything else ready?"

"Yes." It was the woman's voice. "And the temperature is set and checked. No problems. Ready to go."

Hearing that, the surgeon carefully made a shallow stabbing incision that he swiftly brought across Alice's midsection, as if he were unzipping a bag. She reacted instantly. Her body arched in staggering pain, and her scream could be heard deep in her throat despite the gag.

Through her tears, Alice suddenly saw her baby being lifted straight up by his ankles and she could see through her tears, that it was unmistakably a boy. She watched as the umbilical cord was cut, saw the baby get a swift slap across his buttocks and heard the expected crying. The baby was handed to the woman who wiped him down and placed him in a container resembling a suitcase.

"Won't be long now before we're riding the reptile for a payday," the timekeeper said. "125."

"Right. Double check we have everything, and let's get out of here."

As the rear door of the ambulance was opened, the farmer could be seen on his tractor headed in their direction, and deliberately working his way toward the ambulance for a closer look.

"What do you want to do about her? – 145," the time-keeper asked.

"I'll cut her now. With that farmer coming this way, I'll make sure she bleeds out." At that point the surgeon cut both of Alice's wrists down to her radial arteries – the ones that allow pulse to be felt – resulting in a spray of blood in all directions. He then raised both of his hands grasping the scalpel and brought it straight down into her chest to insure her death. Alice twisted in the ties that held her down. Before drifting into unconsciousness, the last thing she saw was the very brown almost black eyes of her assailant as he thrust the scalpel into her chest. Alice no longer felt pain. She felt nothing.

She had a sensory overload that would not allow her to see, hear, feel or process the horror that she just experienced after her wrists were cut and she was stabbed. She drifted quickly into shock and unconsciousness as a car pulled up directly behind the ambulance. It was a perfectly timed and choreographed scene as all four assailants in the squad, the getaway driver and the baby, cradled in the arms of the woman, sped away.

Chapter Two

Joe Walcott saw at a distance that some type of an emergency had occurred on Harris Road when he reversed his GPS course. An ambulance was close to a car in a ditch, and he could see four people hurriedly going to another car he saw arrive. One of them placed a suitcase-like box in the trunk just before the car sped off. Perhaps there was something he could offer to do, and he was willing to help as he pulled his tractor up to the side of his field closest to the ambulance. If the car, or even the ambulance, was stuck, the tractor, he called his Little Green Gant, would be able to pull either of them out. When he got out of his tractor the emergency lights were still flashing on the ambulance, the engine was also running and the rear door was open, but from his line of sight he could not see inside from where he was.

"Hello!" he called out as he neared his fence line. No reply. He called out again without a response and assumed that anyone inside must either be very busy or not there at all considering that a car had just left the scene of the apparent emergency with a number of people. It took some doing, but he was able to climb over his well-made wire fence and looked inside of the ambulance through the rear door to the immediate horror at what he saw. Blood was everywhere, and a woman was still pumping out small streams of blood pulsating from her wrists. Her entire belly was covered in blood, and he had no idea from what he was seeing about what had just taken place.

"Lady, I'm here to help," he said. The woman was unconscious, but alive. The pulse of blood coming from her wrists told him that, but he felt compelled to tell her anyway. Her breathing was shallow, and he took the movement of her chest also as good sign. He knew he had to stop her bleeding, and for just a moment he was at a loss on where to start.

"Start with the wrists," talking to himself out loud. He quickly untied the blood-soaked ties and used them to tie tourniquets on each wrist. That seemed to stop the bleeding, but he wondered if it was because she was simply out of blood. He then went to her belly where blood had pooled where her baby had been. Even then, he was unable to tell that her baby had just been cut out and kidnapped. He decided there was little he could do in that area but, amazingly there did not seem to be much active bleeding there that would need some type of first aid compression. The woman had also been stabbed in her chest, but with all the blood from head to toe, and her still being clothed in that area, he did not consider checking her chest for any further wounds that he could not see.

Joe had now done as much as he could do without more trained and professional help. The woman was cold and very pale. He knew from military experience that she was in shock and close to death. He stood up and began to look for anything he could use to keep her warm. Finally, in an overhead storage bin he found a stack of heavy blankets that he shook out and placed over her. He then held her right hand in his.

"Lady, if you can hear me, I have done everything I can. I have to leave you to get help. My phone is in my tractor, and I have to leave you."

He didn't expect an answer, but again he felt compelled to tell her something. He hoped that she would neither die nor regain consciousness while he was gone in the short time it would take to get to his phone. As he was leaving, he considered for the first time that whoever did this might be coming back. His heightened sense of fear and urgency mounted rapidly on top of what he already had, and he sprang into action with agility he had not experienced for years. In his tractor was a Winchester 30.06 rifle with a telescopic scope and accurate to 300 yards. He kept it on board to shoot coyotes that had invaded the area over the past several years, and based on what he had just experienced, he knew he would not hesitate to use it on anyone threatening further harm. Fortunately, as he retrieved his phone and called 911, there would be no need for his firearm then or later.

"911. What is your emergency?" the operator questioned.

"This is Joe Wolcott. I am on Harris Road, three miles east of Riggs Road. A woman is in an ambulance, and she has been attacked. She's badly wounded and still bleeding, I think. I have done what I...."

"You need to slow down," the operator requested. "Is there an ambulance already there?"

"Yes. She's in the ambulance, but when I found her, no one else was here. No one. I know that sounds crazy, but she needs help."

"I am sending a sheriff deputy now, and he should be there in ten minutes. You can explain it all to him when he arrives, and he will make the call for further help."

"You don't get it. This is no joke. This lady's dying. She doesn't need a damn deputy. She needs a doctor, and she needs one now! If you can't send medical help, let me talk to your supervisor now and I mean now!" he demanded shouting into his phone.

There was a long pause. "Okay. I am sending an ambulance with medical help. Sorry. I must have misunderstood you about her already being in an ambulance, but an empty one. A squad should be there in less than ten minutes. They will be on the way from Henderson Hospital. Can you tell me where the woman is bleeding from, so I can pass that on?"

"She's bleeding from her wrists. Both of her wrists have been cut, and there is a lot of blood. I put on tourniquets which I think slowed it down and maybe stopped it. It looks like her belly is cut open, too. I have never seen anything like that before."

"I want you to stay with me until the squad arrives. Is there any sign of who did this? Is it possible whoever did this is nearby? Are you in any danger?"

"I really don't know. I don't think so because I think whoever did this left in a car just before I arrived. I do have a rifle and will use it, if I have to, if that car shows up again. This woman has been butchered. I mean really butchered. She might not make it, and the sheriff needs to be here. I will stay on the line."

"Okay, stay with me."

Walcott made it over the fence with less difficulty than before, even with the rifle carried on his shoulder by its sling, and he knelt beside the woman. He held her hand which was cold, damp, and limp, but she was still breathing faintly, and the tourniquets were holding, as far as he could tell. Not long after his call, he could hear sirens coming in both directions. The squad from Henderson Hospital was coming from the east, and a Rutledge County sheriff deputy was coming in from the west. Both arrived almost simultaneously and came to the open rear door of the ambulance.

"Are you the Walcott who called this in?" a squad man asked, looking intently at the rifle Walcott also had at his side.

"I am. Glad you're here."

Another squad man went to work directly on the woman and applied a blood pressure cuff to her left arm, then moved on to listening to her heart that also provided immediate information on her respiration before the cuff was inflated. "I need O-2 stat," the EMT ordered, and an oxygen mask was immediately placed over her face. "Her respiration is weak and shallow. I want her bagged with O-2, eight liters per minute." Calling for bagging meant that a device for manual resuscitation would be employed that forces a mixture of air and pure oxygen into her lungs at a calculated flow rate by a balloon-looking device, squeezed, in this case, by the EMT and called an Ambu bag. The O-2 mask was replaced with that device and worked continuously by the EMT.

"What you see is what I found after pulling up in my tractor. Her ankles are still strapped down like I found her, but I used the ties that were holding her wrists to make tourniquets," Walcott volunteered to a physician he saw entering the ambulance.

"I'm Dr. Horvath. I'm an ER trauma doctor, and I heard the call," he said as he carefully removed the tie to her right wrist to see the extent of the damage to her radial artery. "It's as bad as I thought it might be. I decided to go out on this one to see if we could save her hands." Looking over to the squad man, he asked for a hemostat and suture kit. "I think I can do an anastomosis on this one, and hopefully the other one won't

16

be worse." An anastomosis is an end-to-end repair of a lacerated artery and usually takes a specialist to do it. Fortunately for the woman, Dr. Horvath had all the skills necessary for such a repair he often had to perform in the emergency room where he worked. "For a farmer, you did pretty well to stop the bleeding," he said to Walcott, as he moved on to the left wrist injury. It was deep, did not result in a complete laceration and would be easier to repair.

"Farmers have to know a lot more about patching things up than you might think, but I actually learned a lot in Nam. This brought back a lot of bad memories. More nightmares now, I suppose," Walcott concluded.

"If we save her, it's your fault," Dr. Horvath said, smiling with an attempt at ironic humor and gratitude.

"I need the paddles ready, and get on the BP," he ordered the EMTs who were with him. "She's in bad shape, and there's a lot going on here. We're not going to move her until I make a complete assessment, and I don't want to start IV fluids until that's done, but be ready," anticipating the other's desire to move her and get her to the hospital along with an almost standard IV for such bloody emergencies. "Looks like a Cesarean. Neat and clean. Someone stole this woman's baby," Dr. Horvath remarked in amazement looking back at the deputy. "You need to get a crime team out here ASAP."

The deputy turned away and went back to his cruiser to call it in, as suggested.

"Did she ever say anything to you when you found her?" the doctor asked Walcott still standing next to him.

"Well, no. I tried to talk to her, but I don't think she heard me. I told her I was here to help when I found her, but I think she was unconscious and bleeding."

"Do you have any idea who she is?" the doctor asked while he continued to explore what he was seeing.

"Not a clue. I think it's her car in the ditch, and that should help the deputy figure that out. When he gets back, I'll ask him to find out, and maybe he can try to make some contact with her family, if she has one."

The doctor then asked Walcott to step out. Walcott had done all he could do, and the rest would be in the hands of Dr. Horvath and his team.

With Walcott out, Dr. Horvath pulled up the sweater the woman was wearing and immediately saw the wound to her chest, almost at midline and bleeding slightly with what Dr. Horvath diagnosed as venous blood from its darker red color compared to bright red arterial blood. She was unconscious, and he knew he would have to act with or without anesthesia. Without was the only choice. "This woman was stabbed," he concluded loudly, and it was a deep penetrating wound probably down to her heart, he thought. "Not good," he said. "We can't move her, if I'm right about this. We have to move fast."

"Do you think it penetrated her heart?" an EMT asked. "BP 60 over 40," he added.

"No, but if it did, she'd already be a goner. We'll never repair that in time, even if she's made it this far. But I think it just cut her vena cava because of the venous blood and location, if she's lucky, and there's a cardiac tamponade that's probably holding the vein together. So far, I think there's probably a blood clot in the right place, but if it blows out, she'll bleed out in minutes. I've seen this before and we have to work fast. I can't help but thinking her cut radials may have gotten her this far with the reduced pressure, and I'm holding off with an IV until we find out, in case you're wondering. We have to go in now. Get on the phone and call in a vascular. I hope to hell she doesn't wake up." Dr. Horvath did not need to say surgeon. The EMTs knew what that specialist was and also the meaning of the medical term cardiac tamponade. It meant that even with a cut to the largest vein in her body, other structures at the heart next to the cut, combined with a blood clot, were channeling blood back to the heart. That would not last long, if blood started to take another course of least resistance or the clot broke. Any movement of her body would cause those to happen.

Without being asked, an EMT swabbed the woman's chest with a deep purple antiseptic solution for the anticipated surgical procedure. With his left index finger, Dr. Horvath felt along the left side of her breastbone for the tightly bound

18

ligamentous joint of each rib attached to it. That is where he began to cut down and open her chest to expose her heart. If he was right and luck was with the woman, he could make a temporary repair suture of her vena cava, start an IV and wait until the vascular surgeon arrived to make a more permanent repair.

After cutting through four rib joints, he called for retractors that the EMTs held ready at hand. Dr. Horvath quickly placed three on each side of the wound he made, and carefully pulled her chest apart putting her slowly beating heart in full view with no apparent injury, but not the vena cava. It was located at the bottom end of her heart, and he could see that there was a large blood clot in line with the stab wound, and it had not broken loose when he opened her chest.

"How long before the vascular gets here?" Dr. Horvath asked.

"Three minutes or less," was the answer.

"I'm going to wait. If I look under that clot, all hell might break loose, and I want him here to address it. She's stable enough. If it goes south in the next few minutes, I'll handle it. I think we are ready for anything and the vascular should appreciate it. Is that the vascular now?" responding to voices outside.

"No, it's the Rutledge County Sheriff with his crime scene detail."

"Close the door and keep him out of here," Dr. Horvath ordered. "We have enough bugs in here without adding more," he said with a warning of continued germ contamination.

"Dr. Warner just arrived," an EMT waiting outside announced.

"Great. I know him. Let him in."

When Dr. Warner stepped into the ambulance, he could not hold back expressing the horror at what was before him. "What the hell happened? Did you crack her for a dissecting aortic aneurysm?" From what he saw, including a traffic accident in the ditch, that was a likely diagnosis. The main artery from the heart is the aorta and is harder than veins. It can break or crack during auto crashes and is often the immediate cause of death in head-on collisions. The term "dissecting" simply means that a crack is not completely through the artery and allows blood to collect between layers of the artery like a blood blister. Eventually, it will break through, and death is inevitable within minutes, unless treated emergently as begun by Dr. Horvath.

"Glad you're here, Mike," Dr. Horvath said with relief. "This woman was found by a farmer with both radials ligated, one worse than the other, and I found a stab wound down to what I expect to be her vena cava. I've gone as far as I can with her wrists, and I would like you to check my work. BP is steady at 60 over 40, and I have not started fluids."

"Okay. Go ahead and start an IV," Dr. Warner said as he stretched on sterile gloves and put on a mask. He first looked at the radials and gave a thumbs-up sign of approval. He then brought his focus down to her open chest. "This is going to be tricky. This clot is holding her back from bleeding out," he said, pointing to the bottom area of her heart. "When I break the clot, I'm going to have a mess on my hands trying to sew it up, but if it's not too bad, it might work. These damn veins are not like arteries. They're more like tissue paper compared to a garden hose, as you know."

Dr. Warner had a small bag of instruments and he brought out several. One looked like a flat spoon, and the others were various sizes of hemostats. He also pulled out some envelopes containing pre-threaded needles that he opened for quick use.

"You know this is only half the problem. I can't tell what is going on with the obvious Cesarean, but the bleeders don't look too active. Do we have enough saline to irrigate when we get to that?" referring to a sterile solution used to clean open wounds.

"I brought plenty," Dr. Horvath said.

"Good news," Dr. Warner said when he broke the clot. "Just a small laceration to the vena cava, enough to kill her over time, but the cardiac tamponade, clot and reduced pressure has kept her alive long enough for me to fix it. Good thing nobody moved her or this would have been a coroner's case. What I also found might account for why she is still with us."

While he worked around suturing the vena cava, he used a hemostat to reach in and pulled out the broken blade of the scalpel that broke off when it was thrust through the chest wall by her assailant. It caused the remaining blade to veer off its intended deadly course. "This is one lucky woman," Dr. Warner remarked. "I'm making a temporary closure so I can have a better look after we get some pictures to make sure nothing else is left behind." Medically, the team in attendance was in agreement, but they could not emotionally feel any sense of good luck for what had happened to the woman in their care.

"BP?" Dr. Warner asked. "Hand me the saline so we can wrap this up and make sure this gets to pathology at Henderson," looking at the broken scalpel blade and referring to the hospital pathology department where it would be more closely examined and preserved.

"72 over 40. It's coming up," an EMT responded.

Dr. Warner took the first bottle and squeezed it like an empty can of soda pop and poured it in completely.

"I need one more," he requested and poured it in the same way. This time, the void where her baby had been, was becoming more visible.

"Whoever did this knew what he was doing, and I'm assuming it was 'he'. He may have done a sloppy job trying to kill her, but the surgical technique to take the baby was excellent. Not much for me to do here. The bleeding has all but stopped, and I won't even try to clean this up and close until we get back. I think it's safe to move her now as long as we keep her draped and stable. Horvath, I have to give you credit. You sure make it interesting. I think this is one for the books and we'll see it on the evening news. I'll leave her in your care for now," Dr. Warner concluded. "I have to get back but will finish up when you arrive. You are taking her to Rutledge General, right?"

"I'll look forward to seeing you there," Dr. Horvath answered. "We'll get her packed up, and I will stay with her to monitor."

When the rear door was opened, there were at least a dozen uniformed police officers standing just outside. News reporters had also arrived but were held back by yellow crime scene tape 200 feet away. The Rutledge County sheriff, George McGivney, was talking on his cell phone and saw that the woman was about to be removed from the ambulance. The sheriff got off his call and asked Dr. Warner if he was in charge of the medical situation and hoped for a briefing.

"I'm just the vascular surgeon that was called in, but the patient is stable enough to be moved to Rutledge General, and Dr. Horvath is with her now. I can tell you that by all rights this woman should be dead. But I think she will make it. Did you talk to the farmer that found her?"

"Yes, and we have the number for the woman's husband. I didn't want to call him until I heard from you guys. Wasn't sure if it was going to be bad news. I'm sure you understand that," McGivney said.

"I've had to give bad news more times than I would like to remember. I get it," Dr. Warner said.

As the gurney was lowered out of the ambulance, the sheriff made his call to Carl.

"Mr. Simpson, this is Sheriff McGivney. I am the Rutledge County sheriff. There has been an accident, but we think your wife is going to be okay." The sheriff knew from years of experience that he needed to announce her condition generally as quickly, and as innocuously, as possible to avoid the inevitable panic it would cause Carl, if he gave the horrific details all at once. "Yes, that is what the doctor just told me," responding to Carl's first question. "She will be taken to Rutledge General Hospital so you can meet me there later." There was a long pause as Carl asked more questions. "No. I can't tell you anything more, and I really have to go. I will see you at the hospital," and the call was ended abruptly.

The sheriff looked over to his second in command, his chief deputy, standing near him and said, "He asked about the baby, and I couldn't bring myself to tell him. I hope I can get to him before the press picks this up. He told me that she must have been on her way home from her OB, and I want that followed up."

"I'm not sure about the press. We're not talking and the only thing that's out there is this crazy thing about the ambulance and a butchered woman that went out on the scanner and 911 call. That's enough to get to anyone out here," the deputy said. "We do have a lead on the ambulance. It was stolen from Morgan Township. Nobody even knew it was missing. There was some problem with it, and Morgan was using a backup. We'll search it thoroughly as soon as everyone's out. We'll start that search here but will probably have to move it to the impound for final analysis. We'll work up a timeline with a call to her ob-gyn."

"Make sure you get good IDs on everyone who went in. From what I can tell, that would be the farmer, the EMTs and the two doctors, right?" the sheriff said more as a statement than as a question.

"Right. The real problem will be getting all the IDs of the Morgan crew, but we'll handle it," the deputy said as the sheriff got into his car and left for the hospital. By that time, the transport of Alice was already underway.

Chapter Three

When the sheriff pulled up to the hospital, the reporters were also there in force. "Is it true that a baby was stolen?" a reporter cried out. "Is this a terrorist attack?" yelled another. The sheriff did not answer, but the word was out, and her husband probably knew. The sheriff entered through the emergency room doors where other deputies were holding off the press, and he saw a young man with his head in his hands. Intuitively, the sheriff knew this man was Carl Simpson, the husband of the victim.

"Are you Carl?" the sheriff asked just the same.

"I am," he answered, looking up to the sheriff. "They just brought Alice in and the doctors are with her. She's still unconscious." His voice cracked when he added, "And our baby is gone." He began to sob. "We don't even know if it was a boy or a girl!"

"I know your baby's gone," the sheriff said. "I did not want to tell you about the baby until I was with you. We are doing everything we can, and we will solve this."

"Who does something like this?" Carl asked in disbelief of the reality confronting him. "Have you ever had anything like this before?"

"We've had kidnappings, but nothing like this. There's not much I can tell you and, frankly, I won't be able to say much until we find your baby and the suspects. I can say that this was a well-coordinated team effort, and a farmer saw them leave the scene. The press is all over this, and it might be a good idea not to talk too much about this."

"I won't, but why not?" Carl asked.

"It's so unusual, and I hate to tell you this, but you have to be cleared as a suspect. I'm not looking at you as a suspect; I just have to eliminate you as one, if that makes any sense now." It was a smart move by the sheriff to tell Carl early. A spouse is always a suspect in a murder or attempted murder case, and if the sheriff waited to open that door, Carl may not see it as merely routine and become uncooperative.

"There is always some reporter that thinks he or she knows more about solving crimes than we do, and there will be wild theories. That probably will not happen early on. You will first get a lot of sympathy, but as time goes by, someone in the press will turn on you. It sells print and airtime. They always put it as a question: 'Is the husband involved?' and stuff like that. It will piss you off, but there is nothing you can do about it."

"What do I have to do to clear myself?" Carl asked. "Do you want me to take a lie detector test? Why can't I just tell them I'm not involved now? This is horrible."

"You have enough to worry about without thinking about polygraphs. Down the road, just to appease the press, I might hold you to that, but let's just see how this plays out. The worst thing you can do now with the press is to deny any involvement if you haven't been asked. For them, it will be a sure sign that you are. Take it from me; don't ask for trouble by talking to the press. In the meantime, just concentrate on helping your wife get better. I can't imagine what life will be like for her when she wakes up."

"One of the doctors said that won't happen for a while. She's still unconscious and they plan to put her in a coma-like state, an 'induced coma' they called it, in the intensive care unit later. So, I plan to stay here until she regains consciousness," Carl offered.

"Take my advice. Go home; you will be called when she comes around. You need to be strong for her, and we need you to be strong for us with any help you can give. This was not a random event, and soon we'll have to wring you out like a sponge to see if there is something that will help, even if you don't know what it might be. Will you do that?" the sheriff asked.

"I'll try, but I have to think this out. I can't focus on anything beyond helping Alice. We've got a couple of cats and a dog, and I can't even think about taking care of them. I just don't know where to start to pull myself together."

"Neither do we for now, but we will find both ends and the middle eventually. It's what we do, and you have to trust us." The sheriff held out his hand and helped Carl up. "I'll walk you out to your car. I promise to call with any developments."

Just as he was helping Carl stand up, the sheriff's phone rang again, and he could see it was from his chief deputy, Ed Harper. The sheriff knew he was still at the crime scene and hoped for good news.

"Hello, Ed. I'm with Carl Simpson now at the hospital. What've you got?"

"Not much yet. There's a lot of blood spatter, and it's going to be a mess to sort out, if there's more than one contributor. I just took a call from the FBI, and they just heard about it on the news like everyone else. They have Carl's name, too. It's out there along with his job at the University. The press says he's a whiz kid professor, and the FBI wants to talk to him ASAP. Unless the baby's found dead, they're coming in."

"Do they want me to stand down?" the sheriff asked.

"The ASAC is the one who called. His name is John Rollins, and he got the call from upstream. They're concerned this is a big-time body parts case. You know, kidnapping a baby for body parts, as he explained it to me. You might not want to tell Mr. Simpson that. Rollins said he wants to break it to him. The press hasn't picked that up yet, but it'll come out."

"Okay on all that," the sheriff said, doing his best to mask any comment on the body parts theory from Carl who was within earshot of the conversation. "So, are we in or out? I would just as soon be out, if the FBI is all in, but we will talk about it when I get back."

"Like I said, Agent Rollins asked that you have Mr. Simpson call him as soon as possible and also not to take any phone calls until Rollins talks with him. His number is local 801-3404. Rollins said they also have to treat this as a possible ransom case, with Mr. Simpson being some sort of a big-time professor at the University, so ransom is a definite possibility. They want to be ready for any call he might get," Harper explained and closed the call.

"Well, I have some good news, Professor Simpson," the sheriff told Carl. "This case has gotten the attention of the FBI all the way to Washington. My chief deputy just got a call from the Assistant Special Agent in Charge with the FBI in this area. That's the ASAC you might have heard me refer to. The FBI wants to take on this case because of the kidnapping. His name is Rollins, and he asked that you call him as soon as possible. His local number is 801-3401. He doesn't want you to talk with anyone or take any other calls. Your name got out there. I don't know how the press got it, but probably the same way we did, with her car license plate at the crash site. The FBI is looking at the possibility that this will be a ransom case, and I know they will have a lot of equipment to set up. I don't want to be in the way of the FBI, with everything they bring to an investigation, so I might not be involved for long."

"When will you know for sure?" Carl asked.

"Later tonight. When I get back to the department, I will make a decision after I talk it over with staff. That will take a while, but I should know something tonight and I probably will be out of this for now. I will let the FBI know our decision, and Agent Rollins will tell you how this will all work when he meets you. For now, I want you to just call Agent Rollins, go home, feed the cats and your dog and wait for the FBI. I know from experience they will want to meet you as soon as possible. Do you feel safe to drive? I can have a deputy drive you home."

"I'll be okay," Carl responded.

"Fine. The FBI knows how to do this. They have been solving cases like this for many years. Remember the Charles Lindbergh case? That's where the FBI got its start on these," the sheriff said as he shepherded Carl past the shouting reporters, whom both of them ignored, to Carl's car where the sheriff told him automatically to have a nice day without thinking through how senseless that farewell was to Carl.

As Carl drove out of the hospital parking lot, several TV panel vans fell in behind him and followed him to his home where the FBI agents were already waiting. He had called ahead and hoped they would intercede with the press just as the sheriff had done at the hospital. When he pulled into the driveway leading to the farmhouse where he and Alice lived so happily, an agent was waiting next to a black SUV, and ran interference with the camera crews. They could wait at the entrance but go no further. From that point, Carl belonged to the FBI and their plan to wait for any ransom calls that may come in.

Two black SUVs with government plates were parked near Carl's front door, and as he got out, so did eight FBI agents, each carrying bags of equipment.

"Hello, Professor Simpson. I'm the agent you spoke to on your way over, and these are agents on what you might call my rapid response team. We call it the VSRT for victim services," and he quickly flashed Carl his badge and identification as was standard FBI practice. "Have you heard any news reports – maybe on your car radio?"

"No, nothing," Carl answered, as they all moved into Carl's home to get down to the business at hand. First, however, Carl poured out food for Charlie, his dog, and the two cats, whom Alice had named Minnie and Mickey, that were anxiously waiting.

Agent Rollins was the first to speak. "I know you will be expecting a call from the hospital, but I have to ask you not to take any calls until we get set up, okay?"

"Okay, am I a suspect?" Carl asked directly, to get that fear of being a suspect out in the open.

"At this time, no, but why do you ask?" Agent Rollins asked.

"The sheriff said that if this is not solved, I will be."

"Well, I don't think he meant it that way. And even if I thought you were a suspect, our protocol is to get set up for a possible ransom demand as soon as possible. I'm not here to ask you any questions. That could come later, but not now. I want to explain how this works."

While Agent Rollins explained how calls would be answered, recording equipment was set up for the landline phone and Carl's cell phone. Agent Rollins had what amounted to a script of what to say in the event anyone called with a ransom demand. The time it took to say the scripted conversation was as important as the words spoken to keep the caller on the line as long as possible for the trace equipment to work.

"How long does it take to trace a call?" Carl asked.

"Seconds now, versus minutes in the old days. We really had to work at it years ago, but now we do it almost at the speed of light. It's not perfect, so we need as much time as possible for all the cross-checks these guys make," referring to the agents setting up the equipment. That was an answer Carl could understand, and he was relieved that something with modern technology may actually work in practice.

Hours passed. There were calls from his colleagues that he quickly dispatched without explanations. The press called, too, and received the same treatment. There were no calls from the hospital. Most of the agent technicians eventually left with just Agent Rollins and two others monitoring the equipment. Carl fought the urge to ask how long it might take before a contact would be made realizing the obvious that only the kidnappers would know that answer. Carl sat and reflected on the quiet solitude he now had that was foreign to the life he shared with Alice and her constant conversation that made their house a home. Only Charlie, who wandered among him and the agents, gave him some sense of normalcy and comfort.

As time passed late into the night and as Carl became more comfortable with Agent Rollins not asking anything alarming, Agent Rollins decided it was time to suggest the horrible outcome that loomed in FBI circles concerning the motive of the crime.

"Carl, I want you to consider something, before you hear it in the press."

"That I'm a suspect?" Carl interrupted.

"No, much worse than that. It is possible we will never hear from the kidnappers. Yes, we will catch them and bring them to justice, but it is possible that your baby was stolen for its organs."

"You can't be serious," Carl straightened up in disbelief. "Who would do such a thing? Why a baby? What's a baby got that a grown healthy adult doesn't have?" he questioned, summoning all his intellectual logic to his questions to avoid an outburst of emotion to the horror of such a consideration.

"We asked the same questions in other cases with stolen babies, and our medical experts tell us it has something

29

to do with the stem cells of babies that are harder to find in adults. These fetal stem cells are used to treat rare diseases or hereditary problems, and there are wealthy people that are willing to kill to get them. They are willing to pay any price to hang on to life, even if it means killing an unborn child."

"You can't tell my wife this. You have to promise," Carl demanded with a sense of urgency and acceptance. "This is just a guess, right?"

"It is just a guess, but I am afraid your wife will hear it and believe it, if we don't get any contact here," Agent Rollins said.

"But why is that the only other option? Who says they're not just stealing a baby to get a baby?"

"Sure, that's also possible, but not likely. It would be easier to snatch and grab a baby almost anywhere – a park, the grocery store, a parking lot – if it was just about getting a kid. We have those cases, too, and the babies are usually found alive. If dead, the organs are not usually missing. It's babies like yours that are taken preborn and, if found, are found dead with missing organs. It's not something you want to hear, but I don't want you and your wife to be blindsided when she hears about the possibilities," Agent Rollins explained.

"So, where's the hope in all this?" Carl asked.

"What we're doing now is the best hope we have, and we have to ride it out. Even if the motive is to kidnap for organs, the kidnappers might have a change of plans and turn to a ransom demand. At this point, there's no way to know. Something will happen. It always does. We just have to be patient. For now, I want you to get some sleep, if that's possible. Looks to me like you are working on adrenalin, and it's wearing off. When it's gone, you will crash, I guarantee it, so you are better off to turn in now. We will monitor the phones. Believe me, you'll be the first to know, if we get that call."

"Okay. I'll try," Carl agreed.

Carl left the room to the agents who were sleeping in shifts on the living room couch. He didn't believe that sleep was an option or that it would give him a place to escape his anguish, but it was worth a try, he thought, to follow the wisdom and experience of the FBI, if it would help Alice. Sleep did not come easy, but it came.

MONDAY

7:45 a.m.

Chapter Four

By the third day after the assault, a limited part of the story of Alice Simpson had broken on the national news. Once again Rutledge County was in the national spotlight. The Rutledge County Prosecutor, Spencer Tallbridge, received national attention a year earlier by becoming the prosecutor after he made an arrest of his boss, Rutledge County Prosecutor Dan Herald, for murder. The arrest came within an hour before the execution of a man Herald had prosecuted for the crime and sent the county and country into a tailspin regarding the death penalty. Spencer became the hero of the anti-death penalty movement and the anti-Christ for those who support it. Spencer had everything going for himself on both sides. On one side, he was young and idealistic and, on the other, he was young and inexperienced. In fact, both applied and, in spite of his lack of experience as a prosecutor, the governor appointed him to take Herald's place. He had shown exceptional talent as a trial lawyer with instincts and ability that led him down a path stranger than fiction, which could have resulted in his disbarment, but brought Herald to justice. The National Broadcasting Service, NBS, did a program titled "The Farrier's Son" that followed his life from his childhood as the son of a farrier where he learned country logic from his father to his successful investigation of Herald for aggravated murder. A farrier fits horseshoes to horses, and that's where Spencer learned an important lesson that followed him throughout his successful trial practice that he always tried to apply: "Grind to the quick, but never grind into the quick, or you just might get kicked in the head." At twenty-eight years of age, he had avoided that assault.

When Spencer took office, he brought with him a retired police detective, Jake Butler, who kept Spencer on track with questions about evidence that Spencer tried to answer in the investigation leading to his discovery that Herald was a murderer. Herald murdered a young girl for the sole political purpose of framing and convicting a young man for it. He obtained a sentence of death, also as a politically favorable result, to cement his reelection. Butler was an investigator on a similar case with another detective, Brent Prescott, and both always questioned privately the guilt and subsequent death penalty sentence that was carried out years later. Prescott carried the water for both of them on their doubts, and Prescott nearly lost his job by questioning the evidence. Spencer came along as an assistant prosecutor, and Butler saw in him an attorney of talent and curiosity who might resolve questions he had that were unresolved, elusive and, above all else, still on his conscience. After the execution, he never spoke another word about it with Prescott or anyone else.

Herald's trial for aggravated murder did not qualify for the death penalty, and there was evidence, but not enough, to prove that Herald murdered the second girl that Prescott and Butler investigated. A rubber glove reported in that case disappeared from evidence in storage for reasons unknown and may have led to that conclusion, like it did leading to the charge against Herald. Spencer was the primary witness against Herald on the first case, so neither he nor his office could prosecute him. Fortunately, the Ohio attorney general agreed to prosecute the case, and it was set for trial later in the year. The attorney general was able to further analyze the glove Spencer had surreptitiously tested to implicate Herald, and he was able to identify a fingerprint of Herald in the last finger of the rubber glove that Spencer intentionally kept pristine. That finding was expected to seal Herald's fate, but Herald was still pressing for a trial and a rewrite of history on just how his fingerprint and DNA ended up in the blue nitrile rubber glove found at the scene just like the one in the second case that went missing.

To begin his week as usual, Spencer arrived at his office early and settled in to administer justice from the State's point of view with a stack of indictments that needed his review and signature, when Butler knocked on his open door frame unannounced. Butler was one of only a few that held that privileged position.

"Morning, Boss. Did you hear the news about that professor's wife last Friday?" Butler asked.

"I did. McGivney gave me a short briefing over the weekend. It's being looked at as a possible kidnapping for ransom or more likely a baby parts case. He told me that the FBI was taking it over and he was out."

"Good news, I suppose," Butler responded.

"Could be, but McGivney says that if the baby shows up dead, the FBI will dump it back on us as an unsolved homicide and we're going to be late to the game," Spencer explained. "I think what we need to do is at least get McGivney's full report and see what's out there."

"Do you want me to contact the FBI for what it has, too?" Butler asked.

"When did you ever see that kind of cooperation?" Spencer laughed. "You can try, but I don't think sharing is in the FBI's vocabulary until it needs something. Let me know when you get the report. I want to see just how grisly this is, and from what McGivney says, it was a mess out there. You know, I thought I had seen the limit with Herald as a cold-blooded killer, but this beats anything I have ever seen or heard about. Stealing a baby for parts is as cold as it gets, if that is what it is."

"I'll get on it. I would like to see it, too," Butler said as he headed out.

Not long after Butler left to get the report of the sheriff's initial investigation, McGivney called Spencer.

"We thought we had our man Friday night," the sheriff announced.

"What do you mean 'we'? I thought you were out of this," Spencer asked.

"Well, you know what I mean. We are out of it. It's just that the feds had a ransom hit, and there was a trace to Midville where they picked up a guy trying to impersonate the perps. He wanted $50,000.00 and didn't know a damn thing about the facts. Pretty amazing how fast the feds had him. They plan on keeping that case and not send it on to you to add to everything else once they get it solved."

34

"You mean, if they get it solved," Spencer added. "By the way, I asked Butler to get a copy of your initial report, and he's on his way over. Any problem with that?"

"You curious?" the sheriff asked. "Seems like the last time you got curious, we lost our prosecutor, and you got a promotion," the sheriff remarked laughing, considering the humorous irony of Spencer's great adventure with truth, justice and broken laws leading to his new position.

"No, not curious. Just cautious. I don't want to be caught flat-footed, if this gets tossed back to us, and I mean us."

"No problem. The feds got my original, and I have a confidential copy that's not going into records. I'll have a copy for him by the time he gets here. Let me know if you see anything in it. I'm a little curious about this one myself; never saw anything like it before," the sheriff went on.

"How is the professor's wife doing? Do you know?" Spencer asked.

"I heard she's still in an induced coma, and they plan to keep her that way for a few more days. The feds won't be able to talk to her until then, and they're hoping she can ID the perps considering those bastards didn't expect her to live, but I don't think she will be able to offer much. Shortly before they induced her coma, she came to, and the hospital record says she could not remember anything."

"Is that in the report?" Spencer asked. "I mean about them not expecting her to live?"

"Sorry. I thought I went over that earlier. In addition to having her baby cut out, they cut her wrists and stabbed her in the chest just missing her heart. The blade broke off in her when she was stabbed, too. That's not out there yet and not for publication," the sheriff said reminding Spencer of Police Investigations 101.

The sheriff and Spencer both knew how important it was to keep the deep details secret. When facts get out and then a suspect makes a statement, the defense will claim it is a false confession based on what the suspect learned in the press. If the facts are not out in the public domain and a suspect tells something that no one else in the world would know except the suspect, it's as good as DNA that the suspect is involved.

"I didn't know the details," Spencer said. "I know the feds will do a good job, but your guys were there first and who knows," Spencer added, speculating on the unknown.

"Let me know if you see anything. I also want to know how well you think my boys handled the scene."

"Wilco," Spencer said, closing the call with the abbreviation for "will comply." Wilco is outdated pilot talk that both understood – McGivney from his military background and Spencer from getting to know Chuck Smith, a retired Marine pilot now working as a judge's armed bailiff. He was also the judge's personal pilot for his private airplane that takes him around the state for his judicial duties. Being a bailiff was a political position and a dream retirement job for Smith who was able to combine his military training with running a tight ship that he called "his" courtroom. Spencer was on the right side of Smith concerning the Herald case. He liked Spencer's "risk it all to find the truth" approach and had no patience with the political correctness of the new breed of defense attorneys he saw coming up. Since becoming the prosecutor, Spencer got to know him well and enjoyed hearing about his pilot exploits in the military while waiting out jury verdicts to pass the time.

Immediately following his call with the sheriff, Spencer brought up his day planner on his computer screen to see what would require attention beyond the Simpson case for the next few days. Other than run-of-the-mill guilty pleas handled by his staff and a meeting with the county commissioners on his budget, he was relieved that very little would get in his way, if he decided to get involved.

As Spencer was finishing his review, his secretary, Amy Jacobs, gently tapped on his door frame to break his concentration. Amy had been his shared secretary with another assistant prosecutor when he worked for Herald in the felony trial division, and he brought her with him when he was given the governor's appointment. She was excellent in all secretarial pursuits, and she was easy on the eyes, as he often confided to others. He also referred to her as his administrative aide, thinking that the title of secretary was archaic and demeaning to one with such wide ranging administrative and secretarial responsibilities. Like all others on his staff, she simply referred to him as "Boss".

"Hey, Boss, did you hear about the woman who was attacked last Friday and lost her baby?" she asked.

"I did. Not much I can say about it."

"Well, you better think of something because there is a mob of reporters out front wanting to talk to you on camera. Do you want me to get rid of them?" she offered.

"No. I've got this. I'll come out and get it over with. Set them up in the main conference room, if there's enough room."

When Spencer arrived at the main conference room, he quickly estimated that there were eight reporters and several TV cameras.

"Good morning. I am glad you're here," he said disingenuously. "As you already know, I expect, a woman was attacked last Friday, and her baby was surgically removed. As you all also know, the jurisdiction of this case lies with our sheriff or the FBI with all its extensive resources. The last thing the sheriff or I want to do is trip over the FBI investigation, so we are deferring to the FBI in this case for now."

"What do you mean 'for now'?" a reporter asked.

"That answer would only be based on speculation, and I will not speculate on what might bring it back to me. I will only say that if all parties agree it would be best handled in state court, that's what will be done."

"Can you say how she was attacked?" another reporter asked.

"You know I can't at this time. Nice try," Spencer commented. "For the time being, especially until we have charges, there will be no comment on the details that might compromise the investigation."

"Is the husband a suspect?"

"This early in the investigation, no one is eliminated, but I will go out on a limb to give my opinion that he will be quickly excluded. I did wonder who would be the first to ask your question, and I suppose you have to ask, whether I like it or not. I can tell you that this has been exceptionally painful for Professor Simpson, and everything is being done by the FBI to solve this case. When that investigation is further along, I suggest you ask the FBI for further details."

"Don't you feel qualified to prosecute this case?"

"Of course, I feel qualified, but so far it is not my case. When the FBI finishes its investigation and apprehends the criminals who did this, it will fall to the U.S. Attorney or me to prosecute, and I am fully capable of doing just that, if the government asks me to. In the meantime, there will not be two parallel investigations going on – one by the FBI and one by our sheriff. That's a recipe for disaster, and for now, we just need to stay out of the way of the FBI and let it work. I'm good with that. It's not a competition."

Spencer was becoming adept in fielding questions from the press and approached each one with the belief that the questions played a part of the game called "stump the prosecutor" where an answer is less important than making the prosecutor look bad. The game had become a necessary evil in journalistic circles, and to win, Spencer was challenged to focus his answers on what the listening public would find responsible, even if not acceptable to the reporter. Spencer did not feel competent to handle the Simpson case as he spoke because he knew little about the facts, but nothing would be gained by explaining it was too soon to tell anything and being uninformed would be the headline of the story. That was about to change.

After the press conference concluded and Spencer walked into his office, Amy announced, "Jake's back and will be here in a few minutes. There's an FBI Agent Rollins holding, and he said it will just take a minute. Do you want me to put him through?"

"I'll take it; put him through, please," Spencer replied and picked up his phone. "Agent Rollins, this is Spencer Tallbridge. How can I help you?" It was an insincere gesture of cooperation knowing that there was usually nothing the FBI would ever want from him.

"You already have. I just watched your press conference, and I'm impressed. You said a lot without saying anything."

"Well, that was easy. So far, I don't know anything about your Simpson case except for a short briefing by the sheriff,"

Spencer explained.

"I don't expect you to, but I want you to know that Carl Simpson is not a suspect in our opinion either, so you're not out on that old proverbial limb. We checked out his alibi, and there's nothing to indicate that he was involved or had any prior knowledge about what went down. We think it's a body parts case, and we are getting a few more of those than usual. We are still doing surveillance on a possible ransom plot, but we really think that won't happen. The way these usually go down, the baby, or what's left of the baby, will show up dead or never be found. In the first case, it's just a homicide, and we'll kick it back to you with everything we have. In the second, it's an open investigation."

"Until then it's just your unsolved kidnapping case, right?" Spencer asked.

"Better us than you," Rollins answered as a matter of fact.

"I heard you had an imposter last night," Spencer remarked.

"We did, and we are taking him federally. Hope you don't mind."

"Not at all. I've got enough on my plate to worry about without adding that phony S.O.B.," Spencer said.

"Well, I just wanted to call and express our thanks for not tripping over our investigation and to let you know that we all can give Professor Simpson a pass on this one, if you're asked, and I know you will be. If anything comes up on your end with your resources, please let us know. Okay?" Agent Rollins asked at the conclusion of the call.

"You can count on it," Spencer answered as he finished the call and turned toward Amy.

"You want Jake now?" Amy asked.

"Yes. Send him in. In a way, I'm looking forward to seeing him."

Jake Butler walked in carrying a three-ring binder that the sheriff's office put together on the Simpson case.

"So tell me, have you had a chance to review it?" Spencer asked Jake.

"Not thoroughly, but enough to know there's not much here. The deputies did a good job with what they had, but it just doesn't seem there is anything much to work with. Do you have time to listen to what I've got?" Jake asked.

"Why not? I may as well be as uninformed as everyone else," Spencer responded sarcastically.

"From what I can tell, Mrs. Simpson's car was hit in the left rear, which was perfect to run her into a ditch. She was on her way home from her OB; she was eight months pregnant. From what the doctor said about how long she was there, she didn't make any stops before getting hit, that we can tell. There really wasn't much damage to the rear end, just a broken taillight and a little crush damage to the fender. She plowed pretty hard into the ditch, and the impact was not enough to set off the air bag. It was hard enough to get her stuck though, and the car had to be pulled out after the crime scene guys went over it. Somehow, she ended up in the back of a stolen Morgan Township ambulance where she was found strapped down and bleeding from both wrists and a gaping bloody hole where her baby was. Whoever did this wanted her dead and wanted her baby. Apparently, it was a team effort, and she would probably be dead, if not for a farmer who was plowing a nearby field. He saw four people leave the ambulance and get into a car that pulled up. That makes a total of five. One of the four getting into the car was carrying what looked like a suitcase. To him, it looked like one of those old fashioned hard-sided jobs and it was put in the trunk before they left. Unfortunately, he was too far away to get a make and model or a plate number, and they all looked like they were wearing medical masks and gloves because he said all their hands were blue. The crime scene investigator figures the color came from typical blue nitrile gloves used in surgery."

"Don't tell me this is going to be another blue nitrile glove case?" Spencer exclaimed, recalling that it was a blue nitrile glove that eventually gave Herald away as a murderer. "No such luck and their gloves, masks and car have not been found. The sheriff's lab guys searched the ambulance for blood and any other trace evidence and took a lot of swabs for testing, but it looks like the blood is all from one source, preliminarily based on the blood type samples that all match Mrs. Simpson. We will know more after the DNA testing, but it doesn't look promising. She was stabbed in the chest, and according to the surgeon who treated her at the scene, the scalpel broke off and just missed her heart. It hit the big vein going back to the heart, the report says, and he was able to sew her up before all hell broke loose according to him. The broken blade was sent to the hospital pathology lab which is protocol and probably won't show much. The rest of the scalpel was not found. I think that pretty well sums it up. I wish there were more to go on, but it seems this was a professional hit for body parts. Who in hell wants a baby one month from a normal birth unless it's for parts?" Jake questioned thoughtfully.

"I suppose you're right. It does seem like a lot of work just for parts, though. I think I'll get with the coroner for her opinion, if I can coax one out of her. I just want her to tell me what's the benefit of using a baby like that for body parts. She hates hypotheticals. Other than that, it's a waiting game for a body, I suppose. From what the FBI agent said, it might be a long wait."

"Anything else you can think of that you want me to do now on this?"

"No. I just feel that we might be missing something, and I can't put my finger on it. Probably just wishful thinking on my part. I guess I'll just read the report and listen to it. Maybe it will tell me something."

Spencer was referring to his approach to using photographic evidence that he picked up from Herald. Herald was an excellent litigator and had talent that happened to be misplaced. One lesson Spencer learned from him was to listen to crime scene pictures, and not to just look at them. Put them in motion. Everything in a picture got there by motion, and sometimes that motion will tell a story. The same applied, he believed, to reading reports. Everything in a report is a moment in time that, like a photograph, has to be put in motion to tell its story.

After Butler left, Spencer settled in to read the report that was accurately summarized by Butler. Spencer appreciated that Butler's past experience as a police detective showed through his ability to quickly connect dots without omitting critical information. As Spencer was reading the report for the third time, Amy announced that his chief felony assistant, Bill Arnold, was waiting to see him.

"Would you like me to show Mr. Arnold in?" she asked.

Bill Arnold had also been the chief assistant under Herald and required all assistants under him to call him Mr. Arnold. He was cleared of having anything to do with Herald's outrageous criminality, but Spencer, as a relatively new hire in the prosecutor's office, took particular delight in referring to him now as just Arnold. Spencer thought he was too pompous and by calling him Arnold, instead of Mr. Arnold, he would know his new station in the office. It was not lost on Arnold, but he was grateful to keep his job and continue to work as a career assistant prosecutor with continued management authority.

"Sure. Show him in," Spencer answered.

As Bill Arnold walked into Spencer's office, Spencer was the first to greet him.

"Good morning, Arnold. What's on your mind?" Spencer asked politely.

"It's about that kidnapping last Friday. After the Herald case, I didn't expect the county would have anything that sensational for a while. I was just wondering if we will eventually get involved. There's a lot of national interest, if you're watching the news."

"I really haven't had much time for that, but I've been reading the report on what is making the news," Spencer responded. "I get the sense that this is a professional hit, and I'm wondering if the bad guys are mobbed-up."

"All these years, I've waited for a case with real-life mafiosos. You know, the made-men types, but so far no one has complained about paying protection money to someone named 'Paulie the Nose' or being shaken down by 'Big Jim the Knee Breaker,'" Arnold said with a disparaging attempt at humor.

"You've been watching too many movies. This is Rutledge County. We're small fry. No big money here. It's just not worth the mob's while, but I don't think that explains anything about this stolen baby case. Though I suppose it could.
42

No country roads in downtown Boston, Detroit, New York or Chicago that I know of. If the mob, or anyone else for that matter, is intent on stealing a baby and murdering the mother, a country road in Rutledge would be a good place to do it. If it's a ransom case, it does beg the question 'why kill the mother?'"

"So, are we in or out? I saw your press conference, and I was just wondering if that's the end of the line for us?" Arnold asked with a hint of disappointment in his voice.

"It is for now. If it's a dead end for the feds or the baby turns up dead, I expect there will be a pass back to us. For that reason alone, I want to keep an eye on this as best I can, but for now, we're out and you already have enough to do."

"Agreed," Arnold acknowledged and left to get back to work on his case load and the management of the office where he still felt superior.

***

Spencer had a full day on other cases, but the Simpson case was a reoccurring thought. He had read the report from the sheriff a dozen times by now and did not see anything that would answer any questions about who committed the crime. It was the end of the third day following the day of the crime, and he was in the dark literally and figuratively as he drove home from his office after sundown. His drive to and from work was the worst part of his day, regardless of the cases he handled. It was the reality of driver incompetence that was his pet peeve, and there was little he could do about it other than using his horn. Shaking fists and the single finger salute to recognize both the character and IQ of traffic offenders were off limits and unbecoming for a prosecutor. Besides, those actions in these times may well have gotten him shot by a road rager.

It was not long before he was at a red light with a typical cell phone irritation. The driver ahead had her head down when the light turned green, and she was oblivious to it. As he waited, another driver on his right was able to pass forward in his lane, and he, too, was talking on his phone. All this was nothing new for Spencer. He was often heard saying that a red light is not a green light to check market quotes or a grocery list. The ability to multitask while driving and using a cell phone is not a legitimate excuse, he opined, for the addiction of cell phones.

At that moment, he had a flash of inspiration or at least a question that should be answered, he thought. Alice Simpson had to have a cell phone, and when she went into the ditch in a minor accident, what would have been the first thing she would have done? She would no doubt call her husband or call 911 or perhaps even a friend, but she would have called someone. "So, where's the phone?" he asked himself. He, too, was about to violate his own rule against cell phone use and driving, by placing a call to Butler, but he pulled into a gas station to make the call.

"Hello, Butler. Let me ask you. What's missing in the report?"

"Everything is missing in the report, if you want the truth, but I don't think the deputies left anything out, if that's what you're asking."

"No. Not on purpose. But think it through. What is the first thing this woman would have done after being hit?" Spencer asked.

"I suppose she would have looked around to cuss out the other driver, or she might have gotten out of her car that would explain her ending up in the stolen ambulance. What's the big deal?" Butler quizzed.

"I'm driving home, and it just hit me. Every time I'm in traffic, morning, noon or night, there's a driver not paying attention and on a cell phone. Tonight, is no exception. I was just stuck behind one woman at a red light and a guy passed me on my right just talking up a storm. Then it hit me...."

"Damn. I get it," Butler interrupted. "How in hell did we miss that?"

"We're just too close to it, I suppose and by letting the feds take over we stopped thinking. I'm thinking now. What I want you to do first thing is quietly get with the deputy that searched her car and see if her cell was found. There's nothing in the report, so I expect it was not recovered. I doubt they just missed it. Did she simply forget it and leave it at her home? I doubt that, too. A cell phone is closer to a woman than her purse. It's not a case of her not having one. I'll bet my office she has one, and I want it. We find it, and who knows where it will lead? She's just been in an accident and maybe she's taking a picture or making a recording. Maybe the kidnappers have it, and we can get a cell tower location hit from her carrier even if we only have her number. Wouldn't that be great if it leads us to them? Let me know what you find out, first thing. Okay?" Spencer didn't have to ask. Butler knew his question was an order that had to be fulfilled without delay.

Spencer continued his drive home following his conversation with Butler, and he was smiling. Something good had finally happened with all the problems he saw on the road with cell phones. He could now go home and enjoy one of his favorite recipes, he thought, "Four and a half minutes on high and no need to peel back the film over the meal, whatever it is."

TUESDAY

8:00 a.m.

Chapter Five

The next morning, the fourth day after the assault, Spencer waited eagerly for Butler to get back to him with any information concerning Alice Simpson and her cell phone. It wasn't long before Butler showed up with his report.

"No cell phone was found at the scene, Boss," Butler reported. "I talked to the deputy, and even though he looked and recovered every loose item in the car and never found a phone, he said it's likely she had one somewhere."

"Why is that?" Spencer asked.

"Because there's a charging cord plugged into the dash," Butler said with satisfaction and a smile. "You starting to grind, Boss?" Butler questioned.

"A little bit," Spencer answered. "Now we just need to find the damn thing without grinding too far," Spencer said, acknowledging his refrain about not grinding into the quick where he could get hurt. "Any ideas?" Spencer asked.

"Why not just call the feds and ask them if they're looking for it or might even have it. I can make that call."

"No. I told them I was staying out, and this gets me in. Besides, I hate to part with the credit for a great idea. I want to look into this a little further before I talk with them about it. Hell, by that time they'll have it and already have it downloaded," Spencer said with a laugh. "How can we get her cell number? I don't want to ask her husband. I don't want to take the chance he might call it. It's not something we can just look up in a phone book, is it?" Spencer asked. "If we had the number, we could get the cell tower hits for a location."

"No," Butler answered regarding a phone book listing. "But I know where it will be. She has an OB. I'm sure it's in her records there. We just need to stop in. No written request; just a cold call from your friendly prosecutor. Considering the investigation and all, I doubt the doc will ask for an authori-

47

zation. Maybe with a little luck, he won't be there, and his secretary or nurse will just hand it over from her file without any concern. And no questions asked. If he doesn't have the number, we'll have to contact her husband for it and explain how secret this has to be."

"Let's do it. Can you go now?" Spencer asked anticipating that "yes" would be the only acceptable answer.

"Yes," Butler answered without hesitation. "I just need to cancel a few things, but no problem. I'll ask Amy to tell Arnold I'm out for the morning and ask him to work out my schedule. No problem."

Spencer went back to the sheriff's report that listed Dr. Marc Thomas as the last person to see Alice Simpson and included his office address. As Spencer and Butler walked to Butler's car, Spencer began to feel the urgency of his renewed involvement. It would be a 20-mile drive to the doctor's office, which would provide plenty of time to consider his new direction. In his short time in office with Butler playing the part of chauffeur, Spencer was still impressed with having someone drive him around to crime scenes, meetings or even an occasional lunch.

During the drive, both could not help looking at every driver in traffic to take an informal survey of cell phone users, and they were amazed.

"I never knew how addictive those things are," Spencer remarked. "So far, I'd say it's one in three. What's your count?" anticipating that Butler was making a similar assessment.

"That's about it for me, too," Butler answered. "You know, Boss, Dr. Thomas is the last person to see Mrs. Simpson before she was attacked, at least as far as we know."

"Agreed. What's your point?" Spencer asked.

"No point; just an observation. Those guys had to be following her on a well-planned attack, so they really were the last ones to see her. If they were following her, they must have followed her either to or from the doctor's office," Butler opined. "Maybe they followed her both ways. Why stop her where they did? Were they waiting for her to finish her appointment? It does make you wonder, if the doc was in on this in some way."

48

"Could be," Spencer said. "If he was, he's in it for the money, and that's something we have the power to check. Put that on your to-do list. I expect the feds will be one step ahead of us, but it's my job, at least, to take a look just like we're doing, and we'll start with her cell phone."

When Spencer and Butler arrived, their plan was simple – announce, request, obtain and leave. When they entered the office of Dr. Thomas, they looked official compared to the attire of those present, and they were the only men in the waiting area. Six obviously pregnant women were waiting their turn for the obviously very busy doctor.

"May I help you?" asked the receptionist.

"Yes, thank you. I am Spencer Tallbridge, the Rutledge County Prosecutor, and this fine fellow is Jake Butler who is also with my office." Spencer purposely omitted that Butler was his chief investigator. "I need to talk to Dr. Thomas, and I really think it will just take a minute. I know you are very busy, and I did not call ahead. Sorry."

"We are very busy, as you can see, but I will tell him you are here. Can I tell him what it is about?" she asked.

"It's about Alice Simpson."

The receptionist left the room and arrived back within minutes. "The doctor is in a pelvic exam, and he said he will be right out after he finishes. It won't be too long; maybe ten minutes."

Spencer and Butler settled in with the available reading material for which neither had any interest, but it helped to pass the time. It wasn't long before Dr. Thomas greeted them.

"Hello, gentlemen. Sorry to keep you waiting. I probably should have put you in my office. Let's go there unless you want to talk out here," Dr. Thomas said.

"No, your office will be best," Spencer said.

In his office, Dr. Thomas began by telling them that the FBI had already talked to him, as well as a sheriff's detective. "Was there anything they missed?"

"Probably not," Spencer said. "We just need to take a look at her file for some background information, if you don't mind."

"I don't mind. Ordinarily, I would need a release, but considering the circumstances I heard on the news and from the FBI, I would be happy to give it to you, but I already gave it to the FBI. I'm surprised you don't know that," as he pulled out an empty file and handed it to Butler who was reaching for it. Butler quickly looked it over and handed it back and asked Spencer to ask a few helpful background questions. At first Spencer looked at Butler quizzically but recognized the cue to continue to engage the doctor in conversation without recognizing why. The questions focused on trivial matters, and the doctor was happy to expound on his good relationship with his patient and her excellent disposition. While doing so, Butler manipulated his cell phone out of sight of Dr. Thomas, who was distracted by the questions from Spencer, and he dialed the cell phone contact number he saw next to the name on the otherwise empty file of Alice Simpson.

Suddenly, a phone began to ring in the desk of Dr. Thomas. Spencer had no idea it was the call from Butler's phone to the phone with the number of Alice Simpson, and the doctor kept talking as if he didn't hear the ring.

"Do you need to take that call, Doctor? This can wait, and we can step out," Spencer volunteered.

"Oh, no. It will go to voice mail. See, it stopped already."

Butler decided to confirm what had just taken place and hit "redial" for another try. Sure enough, the phone in the doctor's desk began to ring again and elicited the same question from Spencer and the same answer from Dr. Thomas. The generic background information conversation continued. Butler took out a note pad, the type he always kept close at hand from all his years as a detective and quickly scribbled a note to Spence that read, "The phone ringing is hers! Your call on what to do." Spencer read the note out of the corner of his eye as he listened to Dr. Thomas and stopped comprehending whatever the doctor was saying. Suddenly, the phone was everything going forward.

"Dr. Thomas, one of the things we're looking for is Alice Simpson's cell phone. Do you have any idea where it is? Did the FBI ask you for it?"

"No, on both counts, sorry."

"No need to apologize, we're just trying to tie up some loose ends," Spencer responded. "Do you have any idea why she was attacked so soon after seeing you? Was there anything unusual going on like strangers in your parking lot?"

"No. The FBI agents asked me the same thing. I wouldn't know. I park around back and never saw anything unusual."

"We understand Mrs. Simpson was due in about a month, and the gender was unknown to her. Is that right?" Spencer asked.

"Yes. Is that an issue?" the doctor asked.

"No. I was just wondering if the kidnappers had a way to find that out, if they were trying to steal a boy or a girl. Is there any way your office let that out by accident or something?"

"Never. We know that the gender thing is a big deal these days with gender reveal parties and all, so we really keep a lid on that. I'm sure we didn't disclose it. Maybe the testing lab did?"

"Possibly, but how would the kidnappers make the connection between a test result and Mrs. Simpson unless they knew a lot more about her, perhaps from your office?"

"Never thought of that. I guess that's why you think the way you do. You know, like a prosecutor, but we never let the gender out. I am confident in that."

With the doctor distracted by Spencer's questions, Butler hit the redial one more time with the expected result.

"Are you sure you don't need to get that?" Spencer asked quickly as the phone continued to ring again.

"No. I'm sure I know who it is. She's one of those demanding patients that won't stop until I answer, even if I'm busy. I'll call back later."

"No. Please go ahead. I hate to get in the way of medical care."

The doctor opened his desk drawer with the phone still ringing and answered without hesitation or looking down at the caller ID as he brought up the phone.

"Hello, Phyllis. I will have to call you back. Please understand. It won't be long." He ended the call and put the phone back into his drawer.

"Thanks. That should hold her for a while," the doctor said with confidence.

"No problem, I think we're almost done. Do you have any idea, if her baby is still alive?"

The directness of the question startled the doctor, and he flushed red from his neck to his eyes.

"Why should I know that? I mean, how would I know that?" the doctor said with obvious distress in his voice.

"Because you have been listening to the ring of Alice Simpson's cell phone and finally answered it addressing the caller, Phyllis. Jake, you don't look like a Phyllis to me," Spencer said, looking over to Jake. "Tell me, Doctor," as he looked back, "why did you lie about that?" Spencer asked directly.

"I don't know what you're talking about. This meeting is over, and I have to ask you to leave." The doctor was visibly shaking and lost all eye contact with Spencer and Butler as he walked to the door of his office and said, "Caroline, show these men out."

"I want that phone," Spencer demanded.

"Get out of here before I call the police."

"Good. Call 'em. I want that phone," Spencer again demanded.

"Should I get that phone?" Butler asked Spencer.

"Not yet." Looking back to Dr. Thomas, Spencer again reproached him. "I know you know something you're not telling, and I'm going to get to the bottom of this with or without the phone. Do you want a grand jury to tell you to give me the phone?"

"I can't. I mean I won't. You don't understand. I can't talk about this. Do whatever you have to, but I can't help you. Now get out of here unless you have one of those warrant things. I know my rights," the doctor said with some semblance of legal finality that Spencer fully understood.

"Now?" Butler asked.

"No. Let's go. We'll talk about it in the car. Sleep well, Dr. Thomas. I'll be seeing you," Spencer said with a tone of certainty.

Once in the car, Butler could not hold back his observations of Dr. Thomas.

"That guy is dirty as hell, and he's up to his ass in this. We need to get that fucking phone. It's at times like this that I wish we had a wiretap. You have to know he's calling whoever else is involved in this and in a panic right now, so I don't think he's going to sleep too well tonight. He's in it, but probably more a doctor than a criminal. Fortunately, he never thought to turn off her phone. As a doctor always on call, I bet he never turns his off either. Probably just a habit that worked out for us, and I'd love to get my hands on both of those phones."

That was not the first time Spencer had heard Butler drop the "F" bomb, but he knew Butler only used it in extreme cases.

"I agree. I don't know what to make of his answer about whether or not the baby is still alive, but he was shaken to the core, and we need to get a search warrant for Alice's phone. He was right on that. Probably watches a lot of TV. I know you wanted to snatch it, and I know you could have, but if we took it forcibly without a warrant, you know we're cooked on that in court."

"I know, I know. It's just that we were so close to getting something that might lead us to the baby, and I hate to lose that opportunity, even if it means losing the case."

"I had to resolve the same problem with Herald. In that case, there were no witnesses. Too many here."

"So that's the only difference. I thought maybe you got religion."

"Someone asked me the same question in the Herald case. I thought maybe I had before I took this job. Now I've tried hard not to grind into the quick, but I have to say that if there had been no witnesses, I may have raced you to that fucking phone," Spencer said, alluding to his history with moral, legal and ethical conflicts. "I hope I don't get tested again. Maybe we will have to cross that bridge later."

"Well, you know where I stand, and it's your call. Do you think we should contact the FBI with this?"

"Ordinarily, I would say yes, but we don't have much time. They already got whatever they thought they needed from Dr. Thomas, and it will take too much time. That's a commodity we don't have. I suppose by the time we get a warrant, he will have trashed the phone, but with a search warrant, we might just be able to put enough pressure on him to get him to crack. Nothing ventured, nothing gained, right? Anyway, that's my plan and I'm sticking to it," Spencer said with a laugh and hint of resignation.

Chapter Six

When Spencer arrived back at his office, he went to work immediately with Amy to type out a search warrant. It had to set forth in detail the necessary probable cause for the search and seizure of the phone and a narrative of the all-important reason for it. Dr. Thomas had lied about the phone as a critical piece of evidence during Spencer's investigation, and that should be enough for any judge in Rutledge County to approve and sign the warrant.

"What judge do you want me to put on this?" Amy asked.

"Check and see if Judge Macintosh is in. I'll use him, if I can. I know his bailiff, Chuck Smith, and he will get me through no matter what the judge is doing. If I can get this signed in a hurry, I think I can beat feet back to Dr. Thomas before his office closes. I would hate to kick in the door," Spencer said smiling.

"Okay, works for me," Amy said. "I'll give him a call before I type in his name, but I think I heard he is in. But don't you think you should leave the door kicking to Butler?" Amy asked.

"Good point. He'll be with me," Spencer answered.

It was not long before the search warrant was finished and ready for Spencer to take down to the judge. Butler was standing by to do the search with Spencer and Butler decided to double check his office-issued 9mm Glock semi-automatic pistol, just in case things got out of hand with Dr. Thomas.

"Hello, Colonel," Spencer said greeting Chuck Smith. "Is the judge available? I really need to expedite a search warrant."

"He is, and I can make that happen. By the way, how's it going with that Simpson woman I read about? Any leads on her baby?" Smith asked.

"That's why I'm here. I know where I can find a lead with a warrant, and I need it ASAP."

"I heard the FBI took the case over. Are you in, too?"

"I'm in it enough, you could say. We'll see how far it goes."

Smith escorted Spencer through the empty courtroom of Judge Macintosh to his chambers. Such offices were always interesting to Spencer because everything interesting to the judges was revealed in pictures hanging on their walls. In the case of Judge Macintosh, it was his interest in aviation and the plane he owned. Not one family picture was in sight, and he once remarked that those were only kept in his wallet.

"Good afternoon, Mr. Prosecutor. What's on your mind?" the judge said.

"I have a search warrant in that baby kidnapping case last Friday that is the talk of the town, and I need you to take a look and hopefully approve for signature. I also need night-time authorization in case we can't get back to his office before sundown."

"Okay. Let's see it," the judge said, as Spencer handed it to him.

After studying the warrant, the judge asked, "Did you have any idea that the phone was in his office?"

"Really, not a clue. My investigator Butler and I were there just to get her cell number without making a big deal about it. We thought it would be in her file. The doctor gave us an empty file, and at first I thought we were out of luck, but her number was written on it. While I kept the doctor busy, Butler dialed it, and it started ringing in his drawer. I asked him if he wanted to take a break and answer it, and he said it was just a patient that could wait. Butler did it two more times just to set the hook. Finally, the doctor pretended to answer the call as if he were talking to someone named Phyllis. When he ended that pretend call, I jumped him, more or less, and demanded it. He refused, and here I am."

"Were you tempted to just take the phone? Don't answer that. I don't want you to get any ideas that taking it was a good idea, and I would hate to suppress it. I think you get my point."

56

"Point well taken, and I will go as far as to say, that's why I'm here now," Spencer answered.

"Well, let's get on with the formalities," the judge said, and asked Spencer to raise his right hand.

"Do you solemnly swear or affirm that the statements alleged herein for your application for a search warrant to be conducted either during the daylight hours or nighttime hours are true to the best of your knowledge and belief, so help you God?"

"I do, your Honor," Spencer answered.

"God speed, Tallbridge. There's a lot of interest in this one, and I hope you solve it since you seem to be doing police work now," the judge said, as Spencer signed his affidavit, and the judge signed the warrant.

"Not really. It's just that we have a lead and no time to engage anyone else right now. I'd rather have Sheriff Mc-Givney do this or the FBI, but there's no time to get him or the feds up to speed. And I need this now. From what I know about this so far, there is nothing out there that's traceable to whoever did this, but somehow that phone makes the doctor connected. If, instead of lying about it, he just said, 'Oh, she left it behind,' I might not even be here, but he lied. Somehow that lie is connected, and I haven't thought through why he had it, but I'm getting close. When I see the doctor again today, I hope to have the answer."

"I understand. Good luck," the judge said, and handed Spencer the signed paperwork to conclude the conversation and the visit.

When Spencer left the judge's court room, Butler was standing by and ready to go.

"Are you sure you don't want to get a deputy to go along? I probably can get one on our way," Butler suggested.

"No. I think we're good. Besides, I want to spitball this case with you on our way, and a deputy might get in the way of that. I've got you and that's enough," Spencer answered.

"Spitballing" was a term Spencer and his assistant prosecutors used to describe the discussion of multiple possibilities of conduct in complex factual cases to ascertain a factual sequence. It fell into the category of two or more heads are better than one, and that discussion would fill their time while returning to the office of Dr. Thomas.

"Why do you think Dr. Thomas lied about not having that phone?" Spencer asked Butler as Butler turned onto the road leading to the doctor's office.

"Great question, and it has to do with him being dirty. He's involved, or he just gives it to us, no questions asked," Butler said.

"My thought exactly, but what if she left it behind and now, he just doesn't want to get involved? I mean maybe he didn't realize he had it, and now it's part of a kidnapping investigation that's freaked him out."

"Okay, but that doesn't explain why he doesn't give it up once we know he has it. Remember, first, he said he can't, and then said he won't give it up and to go pound salt," Butler recalled.

"Not only that. He also said, 'You don't understand,' but understand what? And that's the part I am having a problem with. I think we need to go back to the basics. Alice Simpson is pregnant, and Dr. Thomas is her doctor. If he's in on this, he knows it's going down after her appointment. He or someone in that crew doesn't want her to make any calls after the crash, so how is that avoided?" Spencer questioned.

"You're right. I know where this is going. He's got the phone, and she has the attackers and no way to call for help. Talk about cold planning, if we're right. After it went down, no one ever thought the doctor was involved, and he isn't concerned about a phone that no one is calling or looking for. If this is true, I'm surprised she never got a call that would tip him off before we show up, but then again she's in the hospital so who would call with everyone knowing that?" Butler opined.

"You have to know that the Simpsons don't have much of a social life anyway, and from what I've been told, it wouldn't surprise me that she didn't get a call. It may have rung off the hook after the doctor's office closed, but maybe not before. Who knows, but I think it is our best working theory so far. We know it's in his desk, so I guess we can assume he put it there and probably didn't know that its location could be traced if left on, but who stole it? Was it him or his nurse? Is she in this, too? Looks like this is getting bigger all the time," Spencer said.

"Or maybe you just think big, Boss?"

It was late in the day, but the sun had not set when Spencer and Butler arrived at the doctor's office. The office lights were still on, and they were relieved that they would be able to serve the search warrant. Butler was especially relieved because he did not have a clear plan on how to break in. When Spencer opened the office door, the receptionist was nowhere to be found, and the waiting area was empty of patients.

"Hello," Spencer called out as a natural and expected announcement. "Anyone here?" Spencer asked, hoping that an answer might come from the office area where they had met with Dr. Thomas.

Spencer started to walk in that direction and Butler firmly asked him to stop as Butler unholstered his Glock pistol.

"Boss, you better let me check. This doesn't feel right," as he applied his detective training and cop intuition.

Butler carefully approached the door to the office area and called out just as Spencer had done. The worst thing he could do, he thought, would be to shoot an innocent employee that might take him by surprise and get shot by mistake. "Maybe it's a robbery in progress of a doctor for drugs," he thought. That was more likely and could be just as deadly. Using his foot, he pushed open the door, and with both hands on his pistol that he pointed forward, he moved in and disappeared into the office area.

It seemed like minutes to Spencer, but only seconds passed before Butler cried out for Spencer, "Houston, we have a problem. You need to get back here, and don't touch anything."

Spencer quickly went as directed and for a moment had a difficult time unraveling what he was seeing.

"They're both dead, and I need to call this in. I'll use my cell," Butler said. "Looks like a double overdose with needles in both of them," referring to the hypodermic needle in the left arm of Dr. Thomas and another in the left arm of the nurse they met earlier that day.

"What about the search warrant? Whatever happened here, I still need that phone," Spencer stated.

"I don't think at this point we can touch anything, but I'll call Mrs. Simpson's number and at least see if we can get another hit on it. I'll do that after I call this in." Butler took out his cell phone and called the speed dial number of Sheriff McGivney.

"Hello, sheriff. This is Jake Butler with the prosecutor's office. Prosecutor Tallbridge and I are at the office of Dr. Marc Thomas over in Blue Ridge serving a search warrant, and we found him and his nurse dead from an apparent overdose. We will stand by here and wait. The address is 121 Oak Street. It's a medical office building. Please call the coroner for us, if you don't mind."

There was no discussion with the sheriff beyond what Butler told him, except the sheriff's closing expletive to describe this new case and agreement to call the coroner. Butler then turned to Spencer and followed up with a call to the cell phone of Alice Simpson. He redialed it from his call log from that morning, and nothing could be heard except the faint sound of the call from Butler's phone, signaling that the phone they were looking for was probably gone.

Spencer and Butler waited for the investigators in the patient waiting area. Spencer was the first to speak.

"Was this my fault?" Spencer asked. "Did I drive them to this?"

"Maybe," Butler answered, "if you're looking for a reason to beat yourself up. I know the optics don't look good, but you did what you had to do and not much time to do it. Hindsight is 20/20. If you want someone to blame, blame me for dialing that number."

"No. I made the decision to call him on it. I accused him and should have known better. I went charging in and thought I had a winner. I guess I thought he would fold like a limp dick. Case solved. I just got ahead of myself and forgot that it takes more than just me to solve this goddamn case."

"Are you finished, or do you want some of what they took?" Butler said, trying to inject a little humor into the cloud of uncertainty that hung in the air with what was to come. Both knew that the events of the day would all come out, and the press would surely make it appear that Spencer and company pushed a good doctor over the brink because of a cell phone that, one way or another, might have been left behind at the doctor's office.

"No thanks, but I'll have to answer for this, and it might get ugly," Spencer said. "I don't think I can pass this off as a coincidence. Remember those immortal words of Kojak that I'm always reminding juries: 'I'd rather swallow a thousand rotten oysters than one coincidence.' Those were the truest words ever spoken by a TV detective and I might have to eat those words after all."

Just as Butler was about to respond with sage advice from years of older man experience, an obviously pregnant woman came through the front door.

"I'm so glad you're still open. I tried to get here earlier, even though I don't have an appointment, but I really need to see Dr. Thomas," the woman said.

"Lady," Butler said with a pause, "the doctor…"

Spencer broke in. "Careful, Butler, I don't think she needs this in her condition."

"You're right," and Butler continued with a revised announcement. "The doctor is gone, and the office is actually closed. It should have been locked. Sorry, but you best leave now because this place will be very busy with an investigation, and you don't want to be here. Are you having some kind of emergency?" Butler asked the woman.

"No. I just had a question about my baby kicking. It's my first, and I just want to know, if it's normal. Are you a doctor?" she asked.

"No, and he's a J.D., not a M.D.," he said looking over at Spencer. "But take it from me, a father of four, the kick is normal and a good sign. You can count on a lot more before you're through."

"Oh, thank you, I just needed to hear that. Did I tell you it's my first?" she said, repeating what she said moments ago.

"Yes, I think you did, and you really must go now," as he showed her to the door and locked it behind her.

It was not long before the first of many uniformed sheriff's deputies swarmed the office of Dr. Thomas. Butler saw him and opened the door.

"Did you call this in?" the deputy asked.

"I did," Butler responded.

"The sheriff ordered me to secure the scene, and I have to admit I really don't know what I'm securing yet. He said I would meet the county prosecutor, and I see him over there. Can you tell me what's going on?"

"Hello, deputy. I'm Spencer Tallbridge, the County Prosecutor, and he's Jake Butler, my investigator."

"Yes, I know. I see you on TV a lot. Nice to meet you and you, too, Mr. Butler," the deputy said.

"There are two bodies in the back-office area, and we haven't touched anything," Butler began, speaking law enforcement to law enforcement. "We found them when we came here to serve a search warrant. However you handle this or whoever handles this, we are here to search for a cell phone. We have reason to believe it's in a desk near the bodies and have a warrant for it."

"My orders are to secure the scene, so I won't be able to help you with your search. You will have to take that up with our detectives when they arrive. They will be here any minute. Okay?" the deputy said deferentially.

"We understand," Spencer said. "We will take it up with your guys, and we'll just stay out of the way until we can do what we came for," Spencer said.

Soon, more deputies arrived along with a white van marked "Lisa Manning, Rutledge County Coroner." By now, the entrance was secured with yellow crime scene tape, and all deputies except the first one waited outside until the coroner made her initial examination.

"Hello, Spencer. What's this all about? Did I hear right that Dr. Thomas is back there?"

"You heard right," Spencer said, "along with his nurse."

"How do you know it's his nurse?" Lisa asked.

"We met her this morning, and we came back looking for a cell phone," Butler volunteered.

The coroner paused on that answer without going further, but it was obvious to Spencer and Butler that she was processing their association with what she was about to see. She had two assistants with her. One was prepared to take all necessary photographs with a professional-grade digital camera and also had a rectal thermometer to determine the probable times of death. That determination would not be precise. It gives just a range, and there is a calculated loss of body temperature over time from the average norm of 98.6 degrees. It depends on other variables such as personal history, body size and air temperature to add to the estimate of the time of death. He also took swabs at possible contact sites for contact DNA. The other assistant was in charge of a gurney and body bags. He provided the muscle to move the bodies. Both were wearing gloves, and she requested the deputy to make sure all others did likewise and also wear booties over their shoes. Those would be collected by the sheriff and held in evidence at the end of the scene investigation. It was a protocol she insisted upon in all homicide investigations in which she was involved, and it was adopted without argument by the sheriff. The coroner disappeared into the back office with her investigators, and shortly after that Sheriff McGivney arrived. As he donned his booties and gloves, he greeted Spencer and Butler.

"Well, men, what have you been up to?" and not aware of the earlier events of their day with Dr. Thomas.

"Here's the short story," Spencer began. "Dr. Thomas had the cell phone of Alice Simpson and lied about it. He's dirty, and he knew we were coming back with a search warrant, and we found him and his nurse dead with needles in their arms."

"Suicide?" the sheriff asked. "Or just a couple of junkies?"

"Too coincidental to be just junkies. He knew I was coming back and whatever he knew, I suppose it scared him to death – literally, and found solace by shooting up. Same, I suppose for the nurse."

"Missed that element of surprise, did you?" the sheriff asked sarcastically.

"I think so," Spencer admitted reluctantly. "I still would like to find that cell phone. He probably got rid of it. We knew he had it because Butler here called her number, and it rang in his desk. I don't know what good it will do now. It did lead us back to Thomas. Beyond that, I just don't know. Probably nothing, but at least it would prove that her phone was here when she crashed. My word and Butler's word won't cut it for that unless we can find it."

"When we get that far along, I'll make sure we look for it. I'll want you to point out where it was, okay?"

"Thanks. I appreciate it."

After about an hour, the first body bag came out of the back office on the coroner's gurney, with the coroner following behind. Her assistants took the first body to their van, leaving Lisa to talk to Spencer and the sheriff about her preliminary findings.

"What do you think?" Spencer asked her.

"I think they're both dead," Lisa responded with intended levity. "You always ask that question, and I have to admit, I have been waiting for an opportunity to goose you with that answer."

"Thanks, I needed that," Spencer admitted. "All kidding aside, suicide or just an overdose?"

"Could be both, but an overdose for sure. No bullet wounds. No knife wounds. No strangulation. No defense wounds. Essentially, there are no signs of violence, and these two are users. Both had tracks. His are on his arm and hers on her ankles, and the one in her arm. She did a better job of hiding them, but he apparently wore long sleeves to hide his. This is all preliminary, and I will be more definitive when we do the forensics and toxicology. I did not secure any of their personal property – no cell phones, wallet, purse and nothing in their pockets that might help with this that we could see in the immediate area. I'm done here as soon as we load up the next one. There are times like this that I wish I had a bigger van."

"If you're done, I'm sending in my techs to go over this," the sheriff said.

"I'm done and, Spencer, give me a call when you can just to talk this over about what goes in my report."

"Tonight, or tomorrow?" Spencer asked to get some sense of importance or urgency.

Almost in a whisper, Lisa said, "Tonight." She waited for the last body to be removed and left without speaking another word.

Sheriff McGivney called over to Spencer and told him he could come back to the rear office and search for the cell phone. Butler was nearby with his plan to call the phone of Alice Simpson one last time. The office was a busy place. The two bodies had been removed, and sheriff evidence technicians were systematically going over the office inch by inch with highly sophisticated photographic equipment that would provide high resolution to detail often missed by cameras used just a few years earlier. The walls were sprayed down with a special solution to disclose blood trace evidence, and the usual fingerprint search was underway with powder and brushes. To Spencer, it was orderly chaos – an oxymoron that fit perfectly with what he was seeing. Butler saw his opportunity and redialed the phone of Alice Simpson, and as expected, there was no answer.

"Deputy?" Butler asked. "Would you please open these desk drawers and look for a cell phone?" as he pointed to the doctor's desk where the phone had been before.

"Sure," the deputy responded, and he opened each one to no avail. "Sorry, sir, no phone here. Is there anything else?"

"Are you going through everything, including the trash, closets, you know, everything?"

"You can count on it, sir. We will be here most of the night. We have detectives now canvassing the area for any witnesses or surveillance video that might show who was here and also rounding up employees that might shed some light. We want to know who saw them last. Do you want to stick around and wait?" the deputy asked.

"No," Spencer said, "but if you find any cell phones, I want to give you a number to check it against. If you don't find any cell phones, let me know that, too. I can't imagine any circumstance in which these two didn't have cell phones, but stranger things have happened. You might want to ask the detectives to focus on the doctor's receptionist. We saw her earlier in the day, and she might have been the last to see them and know whether or not they had cell phones."

Butler provided the number, and they left, waiting for the next shoe to drop. Butler thought it would be the press with stories on the cause and effect of their first visit to Dr. Thomas. Spencer concurred but thought a dead junkie doctor and nurse might get more press attention at first. In the final analysis, they concluded it would probably be both. The coroner, Lisa Manning, also had something important to tell Spencer. It would have to be taken into consideration on how this would play out, and it seemed that she wanted it to be private.

On their return drive, Spencer asked Butler to tune in local radio shows to see if there were any reports of the usual "breaking news" or a "news alert" about the death of Dr. Thomas and his nurse. What Spencer had to defend against in the arena of public opinion took precedence over the call he had to make to the county coroner, and as expected, the radio was alive with sensational reports coming in that were short on facts, also as expected that early in the investigation. The first announcement was framed in the usual way: "Prominent Doctor Found Dead in Blue Ridge," followed by "Drug Using Doctor and Nurse Found in Overdose Deaths." Those would no doubt be followed by TV reporting and the press and Spencer knew it would only be a matter of time before he was blamed. He would not be disappointed.

After listening to the radio reports that had the basics with little else, Spencer made his call to the coroner.

"Hello, Lisa. It's Spencer. What's on your mind?" Spencer asked cautiously.

"I want this just between us, okay?" she asked in return, and anticipated his agreement on secrecy. "Are you driving?" she asked solicitously. They worked well together, and she had genuine concern for his well-being. He respected her role in investigations and that she could not withhold her written opinions from the press as he could, and often did, during the investigation phase of a case. Neither liked that she was treated differently from him concerning disclosures, but both knew they were powerless to change what the legislature had put in place. Only a good memory now between them would take the place of written transparency.

"I promise and no, Butler's driving," Spencer responded to both questions.

"This is totally preliminary, and I'm still on my way back to the morgue, but I am really concerned about what I found in my examination."

"You mean about a doctor being a junkie?" Spencer interjected.

"Not at all. Regrettably, there are probably a lot more like him out there that we haven't heard about yet, with emphasis on the yet. But here's what concerns me. The nurse, Annie Wagers, has ankle tracks on both ankles, and the needle that ostensibly killed her was in her left arm. There was no history of tracks there, and I don't know yet whether or not she was right- or left-handed."

"What do you mean 'ostensibly'? I usually deal with possibilities, probabilities and certainties. Are you about to tell me that her needle didn't kill her, or that the doctor injected her?" Spencer interrupted.

"Slow down. Let me finish. It was looking like it was one or the other as part of working theories. You know – what we call our differential diagnosis that prioritizes most likely to least likely. That's when I noticed a spot of blood a little larger than a speck on the back collar of the white M.D. coat of Dr. Thomas. Otherwise, it was as clean as if it just came out of the laundry – probably did – and I will check on that. But even my husband's shirt collars are not that clean after a couple of days of use. If that coat weren't so clean and white, I would have missed it. I traced the spot to where it would have made contact with the back of his head, and there it was exactly. It matched up perfectly just in his hair line.

"What matched up? What was in the hair line? More blood?" Spencer asked what he thought were simple and obvious questions.

"No, there's only a needle point hole you would find at an injection site. That part you could barely see. You know how nurses always put a bandage over a fresh injection for a flu shot or even if there is very little blood? Well, the shirt acted as the missing Band Aid. Do you get it?" she asked.

"Believe me, I'm following," Spencer answered, and she continued.

"Then I checked the same area on the nurse. She wasn't wearing a blouse with a collar, but a needle mark was just inside her rear hair line, just the same. I would have missed it, too, if I didn't see the blood on the doctor's collar. I have photographed all this, and there will be a complete forensic examination for several things. First, are these needle marks? And second, is there concentration of a chemical at those locations consistent with whatever is found in the needles we recovered from their arms? There's a lot in play here, and I need you to tell me how much of this do you want out. Eventually, I have to form an opinion on manner and cause of death. Was it an accidental overdose by one or both? Was it a suicide by one or both, or was it a homicide by one or both or by someone else? The cause by an overdose is the easy part, and so far, I have little doubt overdose by something will be the cause. Right now, if I had to guess, I think they both got hot shots of fentanyl. It's quick, lethal and I think the whole thing was staged. So, it's the manner that's the big question."

"There's a lot to wrap my head around, and I never considered the 'homicide by someone else' part," Spencer said. "Missing cell phones are starting to make sense."

"I don't know what you mean about cell phones, but please, don't let any of this out except the cause, if it's an overdose. But, the manner, a homicide, I need to hold up on that conclusion, at least until I'm finished with my final analysis. For now, without any signs of a struggle by either one, I can't wrap my head around how they both got it the same way, but that's your job. Right?"

"For now, I'll let the sheriff reconstruct as much as he can, and maybe it will tell us what happened or who did this. Imagine, all this for a damn cell phone that I was looking for. Go figure."

"That's what I am trying to do, and I'll keep a lid on it as long as I can. I'll let you know of any changes I might have to make, and I'll keep you in the loop on the forensics. Remember, and I hate to ask again, keep this between us, okay?" Lisa asked with more plea than request in her voice.

"I promise. You can count on it. Tomorrow I'll be catching enough hell over this without asking for more trouble," and he ended the call.

"What did she have on her mind?" Butler asked.

"Not much, other than it looks like it might be a third-party murder," Spencer said matter-of-factly.

"You've got to be shitting me!" Butler exclaimed, understanding that Spencer was not joking. "How does she figure that based on what we saw and what I assume what she saw, too?"

"The syringe in the nurse's arm doesn't add up with how she uses them. She's an ankle shooter, not an arm shooter, and her tracks prove that. But who knows? Maybe they decided to both go out together, and what's the difference to them at that point. Here's the kicker. Both have what she thinks are fresh needle marks in their hair lines at the back of their heads, and if those are drug injections, their deaths qualify as murders."

"I'm liking the feds in this more and more," Butler said. "I suppose the promise I heard was to keep this quiet for now?"

"Right. It's not final, it's only her preliminary thinking on cause and manner, but she wanted to know how I felt about it. No doubt the feds will be asking too, and I think she just needs to keep this pending for a while."

"Don't you think the feds ought to know? It's their case now. Why not let them worry about it?"

"I agree, but I keep coming back to my involvement in pressing for the phone and pushing for that may have gotten them killed. I don't know, but why add that to the mix until all the facts are in from the sheriff and we have what he comes up with? After all, at this point, the feds won't be any farther than we are, even if this is found to be murder. Either way, the killer will have to be found one way or the other, so what's the rush?"

"I'm not sure of your logic, Spencer, but we can wait and see. All I am saying is that it may be helpful to put the feds on the track of a homicide instead of just the missing phone and the doctor lying about it."

"You're probably right. I think I am just thinking of my own ass. You do have a way of keeping me on track. I'll clear it with Lisa first, but I'll give her opinion to the feds when she firms it up. I expect she will be in agreement at that point, anyway. For now, I guess we just wait till tomorrow."

Chapter Seven

It was now well into the evening, and as they approached where Spencer had parked, Spencer asked Butler if he wanted to take a break.

"What do you say we stop at A-Bs for some fortification before I get hammered by the press tomorrow?" Spencer asked. A-Bs was an abbreviation for the Alibis Bar. It was a cop bar, where off-duty police and sheriff deputies met to discuss or complain about the events of the day without what they considered to be the "unfriendlies" or the not-so-general public getting in the way. It was owned and operated by a retired police sergeant, Clancy Finnegan. He was a no-nonsense proprietor, and no one wanted to be on his wrong side.

"Like you, I might not have much of a life beyond my job," Butler replied, "but I've got a wife, and she expects me home. I'm already late, but if you want to stop by after I drop you off at A-B's, you are welcome. We can try to put it together over some cold cuts and Bud, if that works for you."

"Thanks. I'll pass. I think maybe a little time away from it will work, and I might get a read on the local news, if there's anyone there I know."

"They all know you, Spencer, and maybe a little cop bonding will do you some good," Butler responded.

"Just drop me off at the bar, and I'll either walk to my car or walk home depending how it goes. A walk either way might do me some good."

When Spencer walked into Alibis, he was greeted by several officers still in uniform.

"Hey, Spencer," one called out, "you're in the news again big time on that stolen baby case. Is there any word yet on finding the baby?"

"I've been tied up all day on a lead and haven't heard anything from the feds on what they're doing. I did hear they had a false ransom claim and caught the guy. I was kinda hoping you all might have heard something I missed on the news." "That's about it for us, except you finding her doctor and nurse dead from an overdose. That's the bigger story now. What the hell is that all about?"

"Hard to say for sure, but I can tell you both were addicts. We don't know if that's just a coincidence or what." Spencer had a hard time getting those words out. He didn't believe it was a coincidence, but he still had no firm idea of what might have happened. He suspected murder, but he could not share that with the officers or anyone else until the coroner gave him the go ahead. "The coroner's got it, and we won't know more until she finishes her autopsy."

"How long on that?" a young officer asked.

"With a case like this with drugs, the toxicology results could take weeks. I'd say we should know for sure in a month, but the evidence seems obvious that they both died from an overdose of something," Spencer answered, hoping that would be enough to satisfy inquiring minds for the evening before the news fully broke about his, and Butler's, involvement.

"Who's the good-looking new barkeep? Is she old enough to work here?" Spencer asked generally of those within earshot.

"Careful, it's the boss's daughter, and she's 21," a voice was heard.

"Thanks for the warning. What's she doing here?" Spencer asked.

"She's a senior at Southern University, and she's on her spring break. Finnegan figures it will keep her out of trouble with a job here."

"Oh really," Spencer remarked. "You guys look like a bunch of hungry dogs with no teeth with your tongues hanging out. This could be more trouble for her than Ft. Lauderdale."

"She's good for the scenery, but none of us want to get shot, if you catch my drift," another officer answered.

"All the same, I think I will give her a little warning about you guys," Spencer said with a little friendly sarcasm and approached her to order a beer.

"Hello, Miss," Spencer began. "I could sure use a Bud."

"Very good," she said with what Spencer thought was a genuine Irish accent. "I know who you are. You're that Prosecutor Tallbridge," as she served up a cold bottle of Budweiser. "Have you ever tried one of our craft beers? I think one will do ya just fine."

"No. I'm a little old fashioned. I don't try a lot of new stuff. I hear you're a college girl and home on spring break. This is the first time I've seen you here."

"I haven't been home much, but I'm finishing school, and then I'm off to law school in September. My Dad wants to spend time with me before I start and get me used to the guys I might be working with someday. Like you, even."

"I'm not sure that is such a good idea. I mean about them. Not sure what your dad had in mind, but I'm okay."

"Oh, you're not telling me anything I don't already know," she said with her Irish heritage in her voice again showing through.

"You're right, I'm the prosecutor. All kidding aside, this is the safest place for you on your break. My name is Spencer. What's yours?"

"Kayleigh Finnegan," she said proudly, "and I can take pretty good care of myself, I'll have you know."

"I don't have any doubts about that. Kayleigh is a pretty name. I never hear that name. Do you know what it means?"

"You're a fine one, you are Spencer Tallbridge. Are you asking a good Irish girl like me if she knows the meaning of her own name?" she asked indignantly with her fists on her hips but smiling. "Of course, I do. It's a Gaelic name and means slim and fair."

"You are indeed that, with golden hair and Irish green eyes. You could be someone's lucky charm someday," Spencer said.

"And just what makes you think I'm not already?"

"Nothing, I hope," Spencer said, showing more interest in her than the cold beer in front of him.

"So, what's a Tallbridge? Is there a tall bridge somewhere in your family history?" she asked, without responding to what he had just said.

"I'm the son of a farrier. I bet you don't know what that is."

"Make your bet, Mr. Prosecutor," she demanded.

"I'll bet you a..." Spencer paused and said, "...good old Irish handshake."

"I thought you were going to say a kiss, but a handshake will do."

She's a mind reader, Spencer thought humorously to himself.

"Your father fits horseshoes," she answered gleefully, and held out her hand to meet his.

"Glad to meet you, Kayleigh. I hope to see a lot of you here."

"Me too," she said invitingly. "Maybe you can tell me about some of your cases. As a copper's daughter I learned a lot from my dad, and I'm sure you can add to that."

"I would like that. I mean I would like to do that. I have to shove off now, but I'll be back soon."

"Hope so. I'll be watching for you on TV. That's where I saw you the first time and then in all the papers with the Herald case. Bye."

That was the most inviting exchange he had had with a woman since his breakup with his dream-girl-turned-nightmare. Yet the last thing he needed was to get involved with Kayleigh with the Simpson case looming, and no need to stir the Irish ire of retired, but still lethal Sergeant Finnegan. It was only a few blocks to his car now as he walked along thinking back and forth between the Simpson case and the beautiful Miss Finnegan when a car pulled up next to him. He was startled at first. That was his natural reaction now with strangers, and then he recognized it was Kayleigh.

"Come on. Get In. I'll give you a lift," she said.

Spencer got in as Kayleigh put her car in gear, and they sped off.

"I'm only a few blocks away. I thought you probably worked till closing."

"No. I was just watching the store for Dad tonight until he got back. He let me leave early, and I saw you." Then they both started to talk at the same time saying the same words and then trailing off together when they realized they were saying the same thing.

"I was just thinking about you," they both said simultaneously and realized a connection they could neither explain nor question. Not another word was spoken between them until Spencer told her where to turn to get to his car.

"You mean you don't want me to walk you to your car door on our first date," she said jokingly as she pulled up to his car.

"No, but I'll take another Irish handshake," which ended their first private time together. She smiled and complied firmly.

"Will I see you again before I go back to school?"

"Count on it, but try not to leave early," Spencer said, pushing to show interest without embarrassing himself.

For now, he had to get her out of his head and plan for the problems that tomorrow would likely bring. He would not be disappointed.

***

That night, Spencer did not sleep well. Before turning in, he could not resist watching the local news, carrying the story of how tragic it was that a well-known and respected doctor and his nurse had turned to drugs with lethal results. Addiction leading to death was now a part of the social fabric. Drug-related crime accounted for eighty-five percent of every case Spencer handled, either as a crime involving use or trafficking in drugs or as a motivating factor for other crimes such as rape, robbery and murder. It was a scourge across all strata of society, and Dr. Thomas and his nurse were just fresh examples of just how high in the strata the problem rose. The details of their deaths known to the press were undeniably sparse, but Spencer knew that pressing the doctor and getting a search warrant on the day of their deaths would not go unnoticed. It would confirm what he always said, "In Rutledge County, there are no secrets," and it would not be too long before he would be questioned and dissected like a lab frog in a high school biology class.

WEDNESDAY

6:30 A.M.

Chapter Eight

The next morning, the fifth day after the assault, Spencer woke an hour before his alarm, set for seven. For better or worse, he was married to habit. He made his way to his kitchen and pressed the "On" button on his pre-loaded coffee maker. Next, he programmed the microwave and set it for a minute and 30 seconds for his usual cup of coffee left over from the day before. That gave him just enough time to get out his four-slice pack of microwave bacon and replace the cup of coffee with it. Three minutes on high is all it would take. That would now give him time to turn on the TV for the national and local news and wait for the signal that his bacon was ready. The highlight every morning was the blueberry muffin and banana that he added to his plate to begin his breakfast. It was not lost on Spencer that his morning routine was all that was predictable in his life.

At that time in the morning, the local news was not much further ahead than it was the night before. Still, he knew that would not last. There was more reporting on the condition of Alice Simpson that had not changed, and it was the fifth day following the assault. It was reported she was still in an induced coma, and her condition was listed as fair. The doctor and the nurse continued to be looked upon by the press as victims of the scourge of illegal drugs, but Spencer expected they would eventually be cast as involved in the Simpson case. Finally, Spencer feared, he would be blamed for causing the deaths of two of the potential or essential witnesses in the investigation of the horrible kidnapping. Becoming a cold case was his worst fear, both professionally and politically, and perhaps a result he could not overcome on either count.

By the time Spencer arrived at his office, there was already a noticeable change in the reporting. A "breaking news" report featured a phone conversation with the receptionist of

Dr. Thomas. She was the first to claim no knowledge of the addiction of Dr. Thomas and his nurse. She said that Spencer was there that day threatening the doctor and probably drove him to an overdose. At that point, the press did not make the connection with Spencer and the Simpson case, but instead made it appear that Spencer was after the doctor for his drug use. Faulty press conclusions were the norm to get a story out first and this was misinformation that he could not correct. He knew the warrant request would eventually unravel that connection. Either way for him, it was bad news.

"You have a call from the sheriff," Amy announced. She knew it was unnecessary to ask if Spencer wanted to take the call. Sheriff McGivney had enormous power in the county. He was popular in political circles on both sides of the two major fences and was considered to be much loved and popular by the local citizenry. At twenty-eight, Spencer was his junior by nearly a half century, and he appreciated the sheriff's support at a time Herald still held popular favor before all the details of his crime came out. To Spencer, he was worthy of taking his call without question or delay.

"Good morning, Sheriff."

"Looks like you're in the news again in a big way, and I want to talk to you about that. I'm getting calls that you screwed up the Simpson case. I also got a call from the feds, and all I could do is refer them to you. What the hell happened that got you back into this yesterday?"

"Someone heard about the search warrant?" Spencer asked.

"I got a call from a reporter who talked with one of my investigators at the scene last night. Sorry. He didn't know any better, and he thought we were working this together. I had to tell her I wasn't and had no comment on your search warrant. It's out there. There's not going to be anywhere to hide if that's what you're thinking."

"No. I knew it would get out. May as well be sooner than later."

"Look, Spencer, I would like to help, but it looks like a rookie mistake. You know, jumping in to save the day and screwing up an investigation. When the politicos get hold of this, they are going to want your head. They all got the point with Herald, but it's going to look like you just got lucky. That's the best our side will say. The other will say you're just too young and stupid when you come up for reelection. I expect you will have plenty of competition. Remember what I've told you when you arrested Herald: 'The elevator on its way to the top goes just as fast on the way down,' and I think that's where you're headed," the sheriff concluded.

"You mean I ground into the quick, what I always try to avoid?"

"That's right. Have you at least thought of a halfway decent cover story?"

"I have. A defense attorney once told me in my other life, 'When all else fails, go with the truth.'"

The sheriff could be heard laughing, "That's a keeper. I'll remember it. You might want to think about that when you talk to the feds, because I know they will be calling. Good luck."

The call ended with that expression of hope that had little effect on Spencer's sudden feeling of isolation. This was something he would have to face alone. Butler couldn't help. He wouldn't throw him under the bus, even if he could. Butler did everything a cop-type could do. His thought to call the number of Alice with the doctor distracted was brilliant, he concluded, but the note he handed to Spencer said it all. "The phone ringing is the phone of Alice. Your call on how to handle it," is how Spencer remembered the note, and he made the decision to hit the doctor head on. That is where he had messed up. "Why didn't I just stop there?" he asked himself.

Amy came in again and announced another caller. "Mr. Arnold is here and would like a few minutes if you have time. Is everything okay?"

"Well enough," was his usual answer to this question or any question on his well-being regardless of how good or bad his life was going. "Send him in."

"Morning, Spencer," Arnold began. "I just got off the phone with Agent Rollins with the FBI, and it's about the Simpson case. I didn't know how to defend you."

"Et tu, Brute?" Spencer asked, quoting the last Latin words of Julius Caesar moments before he was stabbed by Brutus and other assassins in the Shakespearian play. Translated it meant "Even you?" After his meeting with the sheriff, he expected the worst from Arnold.

"I'm not sure how to take that, but I want to get something straight, and this might be a good time to do it. While you're quoting Shakespeare, I also know, 'How sharper than a serpent's tooth it is,' that Shakespeare wrote in King Lear, 'to have a thankless child.' You kept me on, when everyone expected you to fire me, plain and simple. I am grateful for that, and I don't forget. From what I'm hearing on the news, it looks like you're in a bad way, and I want to help. I won't stab you in the back or the front either. You might be surprised, but I've got your back, and I'll help any way I can."

"I actually believe that. It's just easier to think you wouldn't and that I'm on my own in this. There are times when I think it's better that way. I am glad you are with me. Herald may have known little else that was good and true, but he knew loyalty. That's important to me, too. I don't know yet how you can help, but we have a long way to go, I think, before this is over, and you never know. Thanks for sticking with me. What did Rollins have to say? Is he after my scalp, too?"

"He knows I'm your chief in the criminal division and called to see if I had anything to do with your meeting with that dead doctor and nurse yesterday. It was easy to play dumb. I told him he had to talk to you, nothing more. I don't know if he's after your hide. He just asked me to ask you to come to his office sometime this morning to give him a briefing. He did comment that the doctor and nurse are of no use to him now in the Simpson investigation and sounded disgruntled about that, without an explanation. That was about it."

"What can I expect from him? I never met him, but that's not new with the FBI."

"I never met him either. He's apparently been rotated in. The FBI does that every several years if you didn't know. The feds don't want their agents to become too cozy with the locals, and it's a standard practice. I would watch your back with him, though. Since the Hoover days, the FBI has been very sensitive to bad publicity, and if you're not careful, you will be under the bus looking up at the oil pan wondering how the hell you got there."

"Oh, I get it, but thanks for the advice."

"Do you want company?"

"No. I can handle it. You just watch the store," Spencer said.

Spencer picked up the Simpson file that had nothing in it, except the search warrant, his probable cause affidavit and the sheriff's report that Butler picked up. While putting on his coat, he called out to Amy.

"I'm heading out to get my ass kicked, and I'll be on my cell, if you need me."

"Aren't you the guy that always says your opponents put their pants on the same as you every day? I think you can handle it, but if you go in like a whipped dog, it won't be long before you're a whipped dog. Isn't that what you said your father always told you?"

Spencer had spent considerable time telling Amy about the country wisdom he learned from his father that always came through for him, and now she was doing a good job of feeding those lessons back to him when he needed them the most.

"Thanks, Amy. I'll be all right. I should survive the woodshed." Spencer was referring to the place his father would take him to inflict corporal punishment when words alone would not suffice to make behavioral corrections.

"By the way," Amy added, "that lady from Dog by the Pound called and wants you stop by when you get a chance. She said it's nothing important, but she has a funny story to tell about the McBrides and Quick."

Spencer had given a Labrador retriever puppy to the McBrides when he saved Molly McBride's son from execution, and he had bought the puppy at Dog by the Pound. It was the local pet shop that was repurposed from the county dog pound and operated by an animal advocate. Molly wanted to name the Lab "Spencer," but conceded to the name "Quick." That would always remind them of where Spencer had to go – grinding into the quick to succeed. With what he had on his mind, that visit would have to wait.

The half-hour drive into the city where the FBI was lo-cated gave Spencer time to think through what he had done and the value of his decision, if things had gone well. He be-lieved he could not have expected the bad result, and that would have to be his explanation. That was his story, and it was the truth. He would have to go with it. There was no other way. Sure, he would be criticized for not calling in the FBI, but as he saw it with the time available, there was no time to do anything else, and it went sour. That would not be accepted by the press, but the FBI should at least understand how he had ended back in the case after he, and the sheriff, opted out.

Spencer had not been to the federal building where the FBI was located. No expense was spared in the marble perma-nency of the building or its furnishings. The Federal Marshals Service was in charge of security, and Spencer approached the conveyor belt for property examination manned by two mar-shals with appropriate bulges Spencer recognized as firearms.

"Good morning, sir. Please put your personal items in the basket and just lay your file on the belt," the marshal said. He continued by telling Spencer that it also included his watch and pen.

"Do you need my shoes, too?"

"No, sir. This is not an airport," he said jokingly. "If there is something in your shoes, we will know it when you walk through."

"Comforting," Spencer said as he walked through the massive electronic device nicely disguised as a piece of furni-ture, but with obvious function.

"I see you're a 'badge'. Do you know where you are go-ing?" the marshal asked, having seen Spencer's badge as a prosecutor on his X-ray machine that Spencer forgot to re-move.

"Headed for the FBI, and no, I don't know the floor."

"No problem. Just take the elevator to three, and you're in. They have the entire floor."

"Thanks," Spencer said as he retrieved everything he came in with and made his way to the offices of the FBI.

When he entered the FBI office, he was struck by how small the reception area was. It was nothing like the beehive of activity in his facility, which had two receptionists and a clear view of the corridors of offices where his assistants worked. It was as quiet as a library, and he could hear nothing of the inner workings that were no doubt doing the business of federal investigations.

"May I help you, sir?" the receptionist asked with a welcoming and standard greeting.

"I'm here to see Agent Rollins, and my name is Spencer Tallbridge. I'm the Rutledge County Prosecutor."

"Is he expecting you?" she asked.

"No, but he called my office and left a message to see him this morning."

"I'll let him know you're here. I'll need you to sign in, please, with date and time."

Spencer complied with that simple request and said to himself with a little humor, "So far, so good."

It wasn't long before Agent Rollins arrived and greeted Spencer.

"So, you are the Spencer Tallbridge I have heard so much about. That was quite a feat taking out your boss and saving that guy's life," Rollins said disarmingly. "Let's go back to my office and talk about this Simpson case and the doctor you investigated yesterday." Spencer obliged and appreciated that the worst would not be shared with the receptionist.

When they arrived, Spencer made a quick comparison between the offices of judges he knew and what he was now seeing. Instead of pictures of personal interests, Rollins' walls were filled with awards and photos of cases that were important in FBI circles. It was almost like a trophy room of solved criminal cases, except for a lone fish that had been mounted and hung on the wall. The fish was next to a picture of a sea turtle. On the desk was a World War II-style hand grenade paperweight with a string and pen attached to its safety pin.

"That's not a live grenade, is it? Is the fish significant of someone who ratted out a mobster and now sleeps with the fishes?" Spencer asked half-jokingly and half-seriously to start with ice-breaking small talk.

"No. It's a dolphin, and the grenade is decommissioned. It's just a paperweight that I use as a pen holder."

"The fish doesn't look like Flipper to me."

"Funny, I get that a lot. It's a dolphin fish and not the dolphin mammal. You see it on the menu as Mahi Mahi. I think cooks named it that way to avoid the confusion. You probably think I ought to have pictures of the mobsters I've put away, but even J. Edgar Hoover had a mounted sailfish on his wall behind his desk. I keep mine here to remind me of what I want to do more often when I retire in the not-too-distant future. This office could be my last white shirt."

"And the turtle? You catch those, too?"

"It's there to remind me of my boat that I was on when I caught that dolphin. I was in an island chain off Key West called the Dry Tortugas. I have an old slow tub of a boat I keep down there, but when I caught that beautiful fish, I renamed it the Tortuga. Keep your nose clean, and someday you might be able to have one, too."

"Okay, I'm not into boats, but what's a Tortuga?" Spencer asked.

"The story goes that the early natives found no water on those islands, but a lot of turtles. Tortuga is Spanish for turtle and considering how slow my boat is, and the luck I have had with her, Tortuga just seemed to fit. Kinda cool, don't you think, naming it after a slow amphibian? Anyway, most boats have nautical or tropical names, and that's the one I came up with."

"The judges I work with have everything hanging on their walls to remind them of where they would rather be. With one, it's golf. Another, it's snow skiing, and my favorite has airplanes, private airplanes."

"I'm too grounded for that. I hate heights. Not too much can go wrong on the water on a calm day and a fishing pole."

"I get it, and I know you didn't ask me over to talk about fishing. I got the message from Arnold."

"I know you did, or you wouldn't be here, and you can guess you're in trouble with me. Let me get right to the point. I made an agreement with you and with your sheriff that your agencies are out of this investigation, and you charge in and screw it up. I just want to know why, and what I have to look forward to, going forward."

"I just ran out of time," Spencer began with his mea culpa. "I just went to the doctor's office looking for the cell phone number of Alice Simpson. Apparently, she never called for help when she went into the ditch, and her phone wasn't found in her car. We figured it might have some value if we could find it, and we only went to the doctor's office to get her number. Her number was on her empty file. You already had what was in it, but the number was written next to her name, and my investigator called it."

"Okay, but why in hell did you go after him. Why couldn't you just let it go and call us? What were you thinking?"

"I was thinking I had a bad guy on the ropes, and I may never get another chance. I put that together in a fraction of a second, and obviously I wish I had that second back. The press is calling it a rookie mistake, but if it had worked, there would be better news. Unfortunately, it didn't."

"Here's the problem, and I want you to think about this. We already figured the doctor was involved. Our profilers figured out his involvement almost as soon as we learned Alice Simpson was on her way home from her doctor. This was a set up from the jump, and we planned to bring him in for questioning as soon as we got his financials. We were in the process of getting a search warrant, too, but not for the phone. We wanted a wiretap, and we would have had it and maybe the kidnappers in the process. We were playing nice with him. We just dropped by to get her medical file and to look him over, nothing more at that time, and we wanted him to feel safe. He ended up not feeling safe, and that's on you. I don't know if I would want driving those two knuckleheads to suicide on my conscience. Take it from me, next time you want to go fishing, call me. I think we know a lot more about fishing than you do," Rollins said looking up at his mounted dolphin to firm up the point in a less condescending way.

Spencer was about to tell Rollins what Rollin's thought of suicide, was probably murder from the preliminary opinion of the coroner. In a moment of hesitation, he held back. He had already made the mistake about the phone, also made from a split-second decision, and he did promise the coroner not to disclose her opinion until she firmed it up. No need to throw that into the mix now, he thought. But if her report pointed to murder, wouldn't he somehow be blamed for their murders anyway? Only time would tell, and the time for that telling was not now.

"Before you go, I'd like you to sign in. Standard practice. Use the pen attached to the paper weight, and the sign in sheet is next to it, okay?"

"No problem. I already signed in once, but twice won't hurt," Spencer said, as he reached for the pen and pulled on the string. The safety pin pulled out, and the grenade handle flew off with a snap sending Spencer into a momentary panic. Rollins obviously had a warped sense of humor and Spencer obviously had a strong heart.

"Gotcha!" Rollins remarked gleefully. "I couldn't resist it, considering you screwed up the Thomas investigation. Got you pretty good, don't you think?"

"Too good, I think. I'll have to change my briefs when I leave. Is that thing real?"

"It's really decommissioned, like I said. It's drilled out, and the primer, fuse and powder are gone, but the firing spring that tossed the handle still works when the pin is pulled. On a live one, you have to squeeze and hold the handle to pull the pin, but I reworked it for a little surprise. It's a souvenir from my military service in demolition. I got the idea from the early improvised explosive devices I disarmed. Real primitive stuff from what we have now. They don't use this old pineapple design for frags anymore either, and the IEDs are now made from cell phones and artillery shells instead of trip wires using fishing line and hand grenades. A lot more fire power now and fewer problems with detonators tied to a GPS signal to ensure a result than an old piece of fishing line with a grenade on one end and a fishing hook on the other to attach it. With GPS, I can set it off anywhere there's cell service and at any time I choose. Just the same, the string worked for you," he said laughing, "and the military still uses trip wires."

"All things considered, I'm glad you have a sense of humor," Spencer said, while privately feeling Rollins was a pompous self-centered ass who delighted in scaring the hell out of people, but not the kind of guy you would want to cross. Spencer finished his meeting with Rollins and left with the understanding that the Simpson case was by no means cold, but there was little the FBI could do to undo the public interest damage caused by Spencer's actions. The best that Rollins would be able to say on behalf of the FBI was that Spencer saw an opportunity that did not work out, and there was no way Spencer could have known the doctor and his nurse were so unstable and kill themselves as a result of being investigated. Unfortunately, the FBI would likely say that whatever the doctor and nurse knew about the Simpson case, they took to their graves. Essentially, that was the truth, but Spencer and then the FBI independently had assessed that they were directly involved and knew they had been hiding more than their drug abuse. Eventually, public interest would turn in that direction, too, and again Spencer probably would be blamed for the loss of suspects and the missing baby. Once again, Spencer decided to stay out of the case and give the FBI any leads that may come his way.

***

When Spencer arrived back at his office, Butler was waiting to hear how it went. Amy had already told him that Spencer was expecting a hard time from Rollins, and Butler had his ear to the ground on how it was all being received while he was gone.

"Got a little time in the old woodshed, did you?" Butler asked, referring to the place a miscreant teenager goes with his father to receive corporal punishment.

"It wasn't as bad as I thought. I got called on the carpet for making a split-second decision when I popped the question about the phone with the doctor, and I suppose I had it coming. If we got lucky, I'd be at the head of the parade instead of being chased by it. What are you hearing?"

"About what we expected. Your enemies – Herald's old allies – say this is what happens when a kid takes over a major office and screws up a case. But the office is with you. Nothing at the water cooler, as I hear it, to indicate you have any problems with staff. We can weather this."

"Isn't it amazing how fast things can happen in such a short time and in a case, we aren't really involved with?"

"Not to disagree, but I think it's amazing how fast things can change when we do get involved. Something as simple as calling a guy out for a lie and we're upside down," Butler said.

"Thanks for keeping me honest about my involvement, but I probably would do it again the same way, even if I had more time to think about it. It's a lot easier to look back than to predict the future," Spencer said. "Any word on how Mrs. Simpson is doing?"

"Still in a coma," Butler said, "and the feds are still monitoring Carl's phone for any ransom demands. I got that from the inside at the sheriff's office, so don't mention it. I know I don't have to tell you that."

"You don't, and I won't," Spencer responded.

Amy came in and told Spencer that the phones were lit up early by the press while he was gone and looking for any comment on the attempt to serve the search warrant and the apparent double suicide that had been reported earlier. "They also want a copy of the affidavit for the warrant and a copy of the warrant," Amy added. "Anything you want me to tell them, or would you like to start returning calls?"

"No, I'll do it later. Procrastination always beats a good act of contrition," Spencer said wryly.

"And what beats a good act of contrition?" Butler asked.

"A confession, of course," Spencer said. "I think I'll call on Lisa Manning and see if she has anything yet."

"Aren't you the guy that promised to stay out of this?" Butler asked.

"I am, and I did, and I will, but I didn't promise to stay out of a double murder on my watch. I'm all in on that, and I'll be damned if I go around with a whipped dog look on my face on how this is playing out. I'm in until I get kicked out."

"Now you're talking, Boss. Count me in, too," Butler said without hesitation.

Chapter Nine

Spencer pulled into the parking lot of the county coroner, saw her car and hoped she would have something to tell him about her preliminary opinion. Spencer liked her professionalism from the first time he saw her testifying in a murder case, and her dry sense of humor was legendary. In that case, a young, newly minted defense attorney wanted to play stump the doctor and began his ill-fated cross examination with the question, "Just how did you know Jackson was dead when you first saw him?" Adroitly, she answered, "Because his brain was in a jar on my desk." After the court room laughter subsided, with the judge smiling and hitting his gavel for quiet, she clarified that she was not at the scene and saw only the victim's remains at the morgue. It was a lesson the young lawyer would not soon forget.

Lisa Manning had come from the oncology ranks and had traded chemotherapy and radiation for certificates of death and county politics. She had heard that Spencer had left the defense bar because he tired of representing guilty people, and she had a similar reason when he asked why she left such a lucrative field. "It wears on you treating the terminally ill or those about to become so. There's no pain in what I do now," she answered. Her logic was always flawless.

"Hello, Doc," Spencer greeted her in his usual informal way when not in the public eye. "Just thought I would drop by to see if you have anything yet?" Lisa was wearing a plastic smock and was with the medical specialist of her office, Dr. Albert Redmond. He was a certified forensic pathologist and an assistant coroner. His daily employment was as a hospital pathologist but was called in to do all autopsies that Lisa was not qualified to perform, as typical in most county coroner offices. Nevertheless, she had good medical instincts resulting from her diagnostic ability, essential in her former field of oncology.

"Good to see you, Spencer, have I got something to show you," she said excitedly and turned on an X-ray illuminating screen. After slipping in an X-ray, she asked, "See anything unusual or anything that catches your eye?" giving Spencer a pop quiz.

"I'd have to say that little white place right here," he said, and pointing to a bright spot on the X-ray.

"Very good, Spencer. You're looking at the end of a broken needle that broke at the odontoid process when Dr. Thomas was injected in the back of his neck."

"I get the broken needle part, but what is the on-what-ever-you-called-it-process?"

"The odontoid process is a bony structure at the top of the spine and is what allows the skull to rotate instead of just going forward and backward. Without it, the spine would not rotate much, and you would have to turn your whole body left or right. Evolution gave us that. Those without it couldn't see danger as quickly as those with it. Anyway, that's my short course on your question. I took the X-ray because I had a hunch that a needle was jammed into that bony area. A needle might have broken there because the one in his arm was broken off at the tip. Sure enough it did. I never would have put it together, but I saw a speck of blood on the back inside collar of the doctor's white coat and traced it to a needle hole in the back of his neck. Dr. Al here did a great cut down to preserve it, and we got good tissue samples for toxicology. On close examination, I saw the nurse had a similar needle mark on the back of her neck. She was wearing a blouse, and nothing led me to her injection there and X-rays showed nothing. The needle in her arm was not broken either."

"You mean you have the broken needle tip?" Spencer asked.

"Sure do. It's in that specimen jar over there," she said, pointing to a shelf in a closed glass cabinet. "It's no longer preliminary with me. We found the same tissue damage in the nurse, and her samples have been preserved with one sent out for toxicology. I've got good photos also. I won't issue a final report yet, but if you want to inform the FBI of my findings, go ahead. I am still at a loss on how they both got injected without any signs of force. Must have been a sudden surprise thing. I just don't know. I expect to have the written report out tomorrow, and I know you could use some help, too, from what I'm reading about you driving this pair to suicide. Hope this helps."

"You have no idea," Spencer said. "I appreciate it. It won't stop the conspiracy theorists from concluding a connection with the Simpson case, but I will now have a little more distance between their deaths and that conclusion. It could just as likely be connected to their drug use and a drug deal gone bad. At this point, who knows?"

"Exactly, it's Sutton's Law. By the way, that Simpson lady sure was lucky from what I'm hearing around the medical association. That broken blade that was found could have been in one of my X-rays."

"The broken blade was recovered, and it's over at Henderson in pathology, but I don't suppose it has any more value than telling us how she was stabbed."

"Not so fast," Dr. Redmond joined in. "You might want to find out where the scalpel came from."

"I would sure like to know how to do that. Any ideas?" Spencer asked.

"What I meant is that scalpels are not something you get at the neighborhood hardware store. It's a specialty steel designed to hold a very sharp edge for a long time, and they usually don't break. We don't sharpen them. We throw them out. What I'm getting at is, if you do metallurgy on that broken blade, you might be able to trace its manufacturer. Might even be able to tell a lot just by looking at it. After that, who knows where it might take you? One thing for sure, it broke, and our good stuff usually doesn't."

"Damn, that's good! Never thought about tracing the blade. Is there anything you can do with that needle?"

"No," Dr. Redmond said. "The needle found in the doctor's arm was broken at the tip and matched to the piece found in his neck. Other than how the needle was used, there is nothing unusual about the needle. It's what you might find in any doctor's office. All things considered, there's no way to tell a manufacturer of the needle, but the blade is a different story.

Here's what I recommend. I'll get it from Henderson, photograph it and send it out for all the testing we can do. It's not something you can do, if that is what you might be thinking."

"Right now, I'm not thinking. I'm just listening and learning some real good stuff. Thanks, and I'll look forward to hearing from you." Looking at a wall next to the autopsy table, a sign caught Spencer's eye for the first time. Now energized with a renewed willingness to learn the mysteries of medicine and its implements, he asked, "What does it mean? What is it, 'Sutton's Law'? Who's Sutton anyway? The only Sutton I know is Willie Sutton, the legendary bank robber."

"Glad you're paying attention around here, Spencer," Lisa said. "He's one and the same with what we do. That's why I mentioned him."

"You're not telling me you rob a patient, or should I say the deceased?" Spencer said jokingly.

"No, and it might be a good thing for you to remember. As you already know, Willie was asked why he robbed banks. Legend has it he said, 'Because that is where the money is!' We use that principle in medicine to come to a diagnosis, and it's actually taught in medical schools as Sutton's Law. It means that when putting together all available information, start with the obvious before working down to the remote. We call it making a differential diagnosis, and it's sort of like the KISS principle you're always talking about. You know, 'Keep It Simple, Stupid.' If you hear hoofbeats, think horses, not zebras. So, it fits that Dr. Thomas, and his nurse were murdered over their drug habits and not your investigation."

"I wonder what Willie would think about making such a major contribution to medicine?" Spencer mused. "Thanks again, Lisa, and you, too, Dr. Redmond. Please let me know when you get any results, and the blade idea is inspiring. Never would have put it together without you. Maybe it's that Sutton's Law at work. So long."

Chapter Ten

Back at his office, Spencer was told his father called. Amy took the call and was told it was nothing important. Spencer knew better. The Simpson case was all over the news, both local and national, and no doubt Spencer's father was concerned. A return call would have to wait, he thought, because he wanted to give Agent Rollins the coroner's opinion as soon as possible.

After being put through, Spencer began. "Hello, Agent Rollins. It's Spencer Tallbridge."

"Hi, Spencer. What's going on?"

"Looks like I got a little cover on my screw up with the search warrant. I just met with our coroner, and she will be making her final report tomorrow that Dr. Thomas and his nurse were murdered."

"You've got to be kidding. How does she figure that?" Agent Rollins questioned.

"It's really amazing. She saw a speck of blood on his collar, and she traced it to a needle injection site in the hairline of Dr. Thomas. She didn't see any blood on the back of the nurse, because she was only wearing a blouse with no collar, but the needle hole was in the same site."

"How is she so sure it's a needle hole?"

"Great question. She showed me an X-ray she took of the doctor, and there it was – a broken needle tip about the length of a grain of rice. It's in a jar now. There are also tissue samples for both, that are being sent out. These samples will probably show a higher concentration of the drugs there that killed them."

"Fascinating!" Rollins remarked.

"I want you to know I will be staying on this case after all, but only to the extent of these murders. I shouldn't be in your way."

"I hope not. Have you considered any motive at this point?"

"No. It's just a guess either way, but it could be either a drug deal gone bad, or it's somehow connected to the Simpson case. It's way too early to figure that out, and there is very little to work with. In any event, I plan to kill the speculation about me driving them to suicide, and everyone is going to love the CSI stuff. I'm going to call it 'The Case of the Tell-Tale Collar'. What do you think?"

"Okay, Edgar," Rollins said, passing lightly over his idea and its association with Edgar Allan Poe's "The Tell-Tale Heart".

"Just make sure you keep me in the loop with anything that may help in the Simpson case. Okay?"

"No problem. Any further developments on the ransom idea?"

"No. Nothing."

"I haven't heard anything about how Mrs. Simpson is doing. Any word there?"

"No. She's still in that induced coma, but I think they are bringing her out tomorrow. I'll be standing by. We figure she must know something, or they wouldn't have tried to kill her. I guess that's par for the course with people like that. I don't know what this world is coming to. Thanks for letting me know about the coroner's report and shoot me a copy when it's released."

"Count on it. Catch you later," Spencer promised as he ended the call.

Next on his list from Amy was the return call he had to make to his father.

"Hello, Dad," Spencer began. "I think I already know what's on your mind."

"From what I'm hearing, you ground into the quick again, but with a not-so-good result. I'm just worried about you."

"It's not as bad as you think. It looked bad, and I was concerned, but I got some good news today that gets me, or should get me, off the hook with that forced suicide thing. I found out a couple of hours ago that they both were murdered, and it was made to look like a suicide. The press will have a harder time pinning that one on me. Someone will probably come up with a theory, but it won't be as bad as forcing them to kill themselves."

"Okay, Son. Just remember to grind to the quick and not into it. Do that for me."

"I will, Dad. So, what's going on with you?" Spencer asked and continued the conversation in catch-up mode for the next ten minutes before getting back to work.

"Amy, put out an email to the press that at 9:00 AM tomorrow I will be making an important announcement here, and they are invited to attend," Spencer said.

"Do you want me to tell them what the subject is?"

"No. Let 'em guess. They will probably think I'm resigning."

"You aren't, are you?"

"Of course not. I just want to set the record straight before this suicide thing with the doctor and his nurse gets out of hand."

"Speaking of nurses, you got a call from a nurse, and she would like you to call her back. I asked her what it was about, and she wouldn't tell me. Here's her name and number."

"Probably has a theory, too, if it's about the Simpson case. I'll get back to her tomorrow. Remind me. Is Butler around?"

"Should be. I'll get him," Amy said.

It wasn't long before Butler arrived, and Spencer wanted to tell him about the development with the coroner. Again, Spencer gave a summation worthy of any final argument in a jury case. Butler was justifiably relieved, having felt bad about Spencer's decision to go after Dr. Thomas for lying.

"So, what's next, Boss?" Butler asked.

"The finding is going to the press tomorrow, and I want you to get in touch with McGivney today so he's not hearing about it in the news first. What he does after that is his business, and there's not much we can do until he brings us the killer or killers. At least we're back in it."

"Do you think the murders have anything to do with the Simpson case?"

"Probably, just because of the timing, but beyond that, it's only a possibility and not much more. I sure as hell won't be suggesting any of that tomorrow with the press," Spencer said.

"No, and hell no," Butler finished the thought. "I'll call McGivney just as soon as I get back to my office. Do you want me to say anything about the political implications that may be solved?"

"No. I'll take care of that later, but I think he will get the point anyway. Also, I would like you to tell him that there were probably two killers involved. The coroner didn't catch it yet, but the doctor and nurse were probably injected with the hot shots at the same moment. His went in his neck first, broke and ended up in his arm. Hers was not broken, but also started in her neck and ended up in her arm. Hard to imagine there was any time between those attacks, and it had to take more than one person to pull it off."

"Nice call, Sherlock," Butler said with a laugh. "Won't be long before you don't need me anymore."

"Sherlock always needed Watson; you twit!" Spencer remarked with equal humor and a backhanded compliment.

What remained of the afternoon, Spencer spent in preparation for his press conference. He called the coroner to let her know the FBI was now aware of her opinion, and he was going to put it out to the press, if she didn't mind in advance of her written report because of the public interest and condemnation of Spencer. She agreed and told Spencer the press could ask for her report after his conference, and she should have it ready. They both had a good laugh over what was anticipated to be a story headlined with the usual words, "Breaking News," and they both shared a mutual understanding they could write the story that was coming.

***

It was a good ending for the day that began with a lot of trouble for Spencer. There was nothing slow about the elevator ride he was taking professionally and emotionally. It was time to stop for the day, and a visit to Alibis came to him as a good idea. Kayleigh was also on his mind. When he walked into the bar, he was immediately recognized by the usual badge-carrying crowd.

"Hey, Spencer. Just saw you on the tube. Did you really drive that doctor and nurse to suicide?" an off-duty detective asked.

"Never," Spencer replied. "Don't believe it. I have a press conference tomorrow to set the record straight. Stay tuned."

"Can you tell us now?"

"No. Why spoil a good excuse to come back tomorrow night?"

"I'll drink to that, Mr. Prosecutor. We're with you, and I think Kayleigh over there is, too. She was just asking about you."

"Well, I guess I'll have to find out what the little lady wanted," Spencer said as he walked over to the bar where Kayleigh was busy mixing a colorful concoction worthy of a chemistry award.

"Hi, Spencer," she said without looking up from the task at hand. "I was wondering when you might be back."

"Any chance you missed me?" he asked cautiously and without betraying how much he missed her.

"Absolutely not. How could I miss you? You're all over the TV, and I don't think they are being very nice to you."

"'Nice' is not a part of their job description. Last year they all loved me, but today, well, not so much."

"When you walked in, I heard that might change tomorrow."

"You must have missed me a little to be interested in that news."

"No. I heard it just a few minutes ago, and I'm interested in what's going on. That's all. I did like our first date though," she said, smiling and letting on slightly that she did miss Spencer and cared about what was happening to him.

"Tell me, Kayleigh, why do you want to become a lawyer?"

"I didn't at first. I thought maybe a teacher would be a good fit. Then I started following the Herald case and when you saved McBride's life..." she choked up just a little and

97

could not complete the thought. It was enough for Spencer to know he had made a good impression on Kayleigh. "My dad was not too happy about it at first. He called you Mr. Showboat for a while, but that's changed, I think. When I told him that I was changing my major to pre-law, I think he knew you were behind it. That's why I am worried about you being blamed for the suicide of those two. I don't want my dad to be disappointed in you. Does that make any sense, or am I just talking too much?"

"It makes sense to me," he said softly. "I want you to know I missed you after what you call our first date," he said. "Hey, what kind of a bartender are you anyway? Aren't I the one who's supposed to do all the talking and you providing all the bartender therapy?"

"Okay, if that's the way you want it. What's on your mind, Spencer?"

Summoning all the courage he could muster, he said "You are. You're special. I knew it the first time I saw you. I wasn't sure if I was just looking for an escape from hitting a bad patch or what, but you're special. I know that's probably the worst pick-up line you've ever heard, but it's the truth, and that's it."

"What's 'it'?" she asked.

"I want to get to know you, spend time with you and not get shot by your dad. Is that asking too much?"

"Not on the first two, but you might have to work on the not getting shot part," she said encouragingly.

As Spencer was about to go further, an off-duty patrol officer came over interrupting the private moment shared by Spencer and Kayleigh.

"Prosecutor Tallbridge, I'm Jim Fields, and no matter what anyone says, I think you're doing a great job. At twenty-eight, they said you're too young for the job, but they can't argue with results regardless of how old you are, even with what's in the news."

"Don't worry about that suicide thing. It's going away tomorrow, and I'm not," Spencer said to dispel any notion in the rumor mill that he might resign.

"Glad to hear it. How is that Simpson lady doing, if you know?"

"I hear she is doing much better, and she might regain consciousness tomorrow."

"Sure was lucky Joe Walcott came along. I've known him for years. He's a tough old dude. He was a tough guy before he went to Vietnam and even tougher when he got back. He did two tours as an Army Ranger. I call him G.I. Joe. When I heard about the incident, I went out to see him. He's the kind of guy you want watching your back."

"Did he tell you about the rifle he had with him?" Spencer asked.

"Sure did. Those bastards were lucky they didn't have a run-in with him. Four against him and they lose. He's a good shot, but his heart is with parachutes. He was in the Airborne Division. Never could figure out why he likes to jump out of a perfectly good airplane. After what went on in Nam, I often wonder if he has a death wish."

"How does he like farming?"

"When he came back from Nam, he didn't say much and still hasn't said too much about farming or his service. He's been a stay-to-himself type for the most part since he came home, and he says the isolation out in the middle of a grain field away from everyone suits him just fine. But he is a take-charge kind of guy in a pinch, and I think he proved it. From what I hear, he saved her life."

"He sure as hell gave her a good start, and the doctors did the rest. Without him, she would be dead for sure."

Sergeant Finnegan came through the kitchen door carrying a tray of steak sandwiches.

"Hello, Spencer. Glad to see you taking a little time off for a change. My daughter wouldn't have anything to do with that would she? Have a sandwich; I started these when I saw you come in."

"Can you blame me, Sarge?" Spencer asked, turning the question right back on Finnegan and deflecting what would have been a pointed confession.

"Not at all, Spencer. I hope to see you here more often."

The implication of 'here' in that answer was not lost on Spencer. He would have to see Kayleigh at the bar and a second date, as far as Finnegan was concerned, was not out of the question. Spencer did not turn down the sandwich, and it beat anything he had at his apartment. Judging there was little opportunity for more therapy from Kayleigh, he left her with the well-received promise to return.

As he turned to leave, she asked, "Are you parked very far away?"

"Regrettably, no. See you soon."

100

THURSDAY

9:00 A.M.

Chapter Eleven

The next morning, the sixth day after the assault, Spencer was ready to enter what he called the lion's den. His conference room was packed with TV cameras and reporters ready to dissect him where he was standing between the American and Ohio flags that flanked him. It would be payback for what the media perceived as his attack leading to double suicides. To the media, the drug addiction of the doctor and his nurse was only a secondary concern. To reporters, they were merely victims of bad choices, and Spencer had wrongfully and cruelly pushed them over the edge. In their eyes, he had to be held accountable. They, too, intended to add their measure of pressure upon Spencer, and his reaction would continue to sell what the media were offering.

"Good morning," Spencer began. "Thank you for coming." The lights were almost blinding. It was a real-life version of the third degree of old movie lore and reading any notes would have been difficult. Spencer knew his script and would not miss a beat. "I have read your reports, and I have to admit disappointment. Not with me, but with all of you." When he spoke those words to set the tone of what was to follow, a groan was heard coming uniformly throughout the many present. "You have made your accusations against me about causing the deaths of the doctor and his nurse. I have called this meeting with you to set the record straight. Dr. Thomas and his nurse did not commit suicide; they were murdered, and it was made to look like a suicide. That is not just my opinion, but the opinion of our Rutledge County Coroner, Dr. Lisa Manning, and our forensic pathologist, Dr. Albert Redmond. Their reports will be available today, and I recommend you read them. What happened to them is fascinating and equally tragic. I don't know why they were murdered, but I have to tell you this: I didn't push them over the edge, as you all seem to claim." Spencer was immediately interrupted before he could go further with several reporters talking incoherently at once. "Hold on," Spencer attempted to continue. "One at a time, please."

"Didn't you go to his office because he lied about having the Simpson phone?" a reporter asked.

"Glad you brought that up. I did go there for that purpose, because there was no time to do anything else, in my opinion. I have a lady in a coma, and her baby was kidnapped. Stolen might be more appropriate vernacular. If there was any chance of making any connection between Mrs. Simpson and Dr. Thomas beyond a purely patient/doctor relationship, I had to act fast. Who would have guessed that the doctor was involved in drugs along with his nurse? I get that you drew your conclusions, but the facts prove them wrong. Is hindsight 20/20? Sure it is, but any delay in finding the Simpson baby is something I would not want to live with."

"Do you think their deaths are connected to the Simpson case?"

"I don't have any evidence that they are. It's an empty conclusion for now, but I can tell you for certain, beyond any reasonable doubt, that their deaths were murder and not suicide. I'm staying on that case now, and the FBI is doing its job on the kidnapping. I'll be staying out of that, but on the murders, count me in and the sheriff, too. Thank you all for coming."

With that concluding remark, Spencer stepped off the small podium and left the room with no further comment, and no further questions were asked. There was as mutual understanding that the conference was over. Spencer made it clear he was not happy with them, and they now had a "bombshell" story to get out with a "news alert" concerning the new angle on the death of the doctor and his nurse. It was a win for both sides. There would be no apologies, and the reporters were forced to conclude that Spencer was not at fault, at least for now.

When Spencer returned to his office, Amy asked, "Do you want me to get the nurse that called yesterday on the phone? You did ask me to remind you. Her name is Teresa

Rowland, and she said it's important."

"Everything around here is important," Spencer said dismissively. "Go ahead. I'll talk with her."

"It's ringing," Amy said, and Spencer picked up the phone.

"Hello, this is Spencer Tallbridge, the Prosecutor. Is this Teresa Rowland?"

"It is. I'm an ER nurse at Rutledge, and I was on duty when the Simpson lady was brought in. I really need to talk to you. I don't want to, but I don't know where else to turn. She's being brought out of her coma soon, and I'm afraid. I'm afraid for her. I know you're fair and want to help. Can we talk?"

"Sure. Go ahead."

"Not over the phone. Can you come to the hospital now?"

"The best I can do is one o'clock, if that works for you."

"I guess it will have to. I will meet you at one at the information counter, but please don't mention my name, if you get there before me. Okay?"

"Okay. I'll just wait there until you introduce yourself."

"Thanks. Bye," she said, ending the call.

Spencer rocked back in his desk chair and tried to put together this new information with the Simpson case. There would be no time for delay, and he called out to his secretary to adjust his schedule.

"Amy, I'll be taking a late lunch. I'm meeting that nurse at the hospital at one, and I don't know how long it will take. It's probably nothing, but she said the magic word, 'Simpson.' I'll be on my cell, if you need me, but I won't be leaving for a couple of hours."

"Good thing," she said. "The sheriff is at the front desk and wants to talk with you."

"Just when I thought I was going to get a breather. Bring him back," Spencer said.

"Good morning, old friend," Spencer began as the sheriff arrived. "I know you got word from Butler about the coroner's opinion."

"I did, and I would like to know your thoughts on how to proceed because, frankly, we don't have jack shit!"

"I know. First, it's a couple of suicides, and now it's a double homicide. The coroner is looking at that broken blade and might give us something, but beyond what you might turn up from the ambulance you searched, I don't know where to start either," Spencer said.

"My guys are telling me it's as clean as the driven snow. Nothing of value. No prints. Nothing left behind. No DNA probably, except the DNA of Mrs. Simpson. No witnesses, except that farmer who can't identify anything like the make and model of the car that was driving away or the four getting in it. And, of course, that lying dead doctor and the missing cell phone. What do you want me to say since you got us both back into this mess?"

"Tell whomever that we're still waiting on the DNA from the scene. It's true, and that delay will give us some time."

"Time for what?" the sheriff asked.

"Time for Spencer's Law to kick in," Spencer said with a laugh.

"Never heard of that one. What the hell is it?"

"In my other life as a defense attorney, I always got a lot of flak for saying, 'Just wait. If we wait long enough, something bad will always happen to the other side.' They ended up calling it Spencer's Law because, when I was involved, something always seemed to happen to screw up the other side."

"Aren't you forgetting that we are the 'other side'?"

"No. It's my law, and I say it applies. Be patient and hope for the best."

"Glad I came over for a dose of hope. By the way, I saw your press conference. Nice job. I think you're off the hook with our local politicians, but we still need some of that hope you're dishing out."

"I'll be working on it right along with you. Let me know if your detectives can come up with something once all this sinks in. It's early. I think we have time before it starts looking cold to the press. We also want you to know that there were at least two killers, and your guys are looking for the cell phones of the doctor and nurse, as well as the one for Mrs. Simpson. Any one of those phones might be traceable, if still on. The hot shots were probably given simultaneously because of the way they were found, and no one person could have pulled that off."

"Thanks. I'll look into all that and keep you in the loop. It's still early, and we might get lucky," the sheriff said as he moved toward the door along with Spencer to show him out.

The sheriff left, and Spencer was finally able to turn his attention to something, anything, other than what he was now calling the Thomas murders, but that was not to last. As Spencer walked past Amy's desk, she was taking a call.

"It's the coroner for you. I suppose you'll want to take it," Amy announced.

"Of course, put her through."

"Hello, Doc. What's going on in your world?"

"I went over to the hospital this morning, just out of curiosity, because they were bringing Mrs. Simpson out of her induced coma. It went very well. The FBI guys were there, too, looking all businesslike in their oversized blue suits. Is that a standard for them?"

"It would scare you if you knew what was under those bulky blue suits," Spencer said.

"I wasn't in the room, but when she came around, she couldn't remember anything about what happened or who did it to her. She did remember one thing. She had heard her baby crying and asked for her baby, not from the bad guys, but from her husband, who was there beside her hospital bed. It was a horrible moment for her when Carl told her. The doctor's wanted him there to soften the blow when she found out, if she didn't know. I talked to one of my colleagues about the memory loss. He told me it could be permanent or temporary. He said remembering the baby crying is explained psychologically as retaining the one good thing that happened to her. Everything else is repressed."

"Are they sure she's not just holding back what happened?"

"They're positive," Dr. Manning said. "I also talked to Dr. Redmond this morning. He went over to Henderson and checked out that broken blade for testing. He said there are features that you might find interesting, and he asked me to have you give him a call. You should have his lab number."

"I do and thanks. I'll give him a call now. How is Mrs. Simpson doing?"

"That's like asking Mrs. Lincoln, 'Other than that, how did you like the play?' Let's just say she survived a close call, and she'll make it. How she handles this is the real unknown, but I'll keep you posted when I hear anything else. I wouldn't expect her to be walking for a week."

"Okay. Thanks. I'll look forward to hearing from you and more of your graveyard humor, as always," Spencer said.

Spencer now had one more call to make before he could tackle administrative tasks, which were piling up. Being a prosecutor was not all it was cracked up to be, he now learned from experience, except the obvious power of the position. He could delegate every case in his office to assistants, but the daily chores of running the business of prosecution was all his and a time killer. Working the Thomas murders was a welcomed diversion but was now beginning to take its toll on him with little, if any, progress to show for it.

"Amy, I need you to get Dr. Redmond on the phone," Spencer called out. "He's under the coroner in your directory."

"Got it. It's dialing now and pick up, if you want to."

"Hello, Dr. Redmond, it's Spencer Tallbridge. Dr. Manning told me to give you a call about that scalpel blade, and that you examined it."

"I did, I did," the doctor answered excitedly. "I don't know what it might mean to you, but I've got an opinion on the blade, just from its appearance."

"Okay," Spencer said. "You've certainly got my attention, and I think anything will help."

"You need to know a little about scalpels. It has been one of the most important pieces of medical equipment going back literally thousands of years. The earliest ones were found in caves made of sharpened stone. Roman soldiers carried small metal ones they called scalpellis. That's where the name comes from. In more modern times, they were made in one piece and made of silver, nickel or stainless steel, as far as the metal ones are concerned. Today, scalpels are made with detachable blades, and this blade is from a single piece of metal. The blade is also tarnished and is probably made

107

of nickel. We now use detachable stainless blades that don't tarnish because stainless blades all have high carbon content for strength and sharpness. They don't break. Nickel does. I couldn't even find a place to buy a scalpel with this blade, but I could overseas. When I worked with our troops in Iraq, this was the blade shape the Iraqis used. We wouldn't touch them. Looked bad and dull. I'm not saying this came from Iraq, but it wasn't made by any suppliers here in the States or by our British supplier. This came from the Middle East, anywhere starting from Syria and going east from there and probably ending at the Indian border. By the way, I'm not including Israel. They use our stuff."

"Are you sure about the metal?"

"I'm sure it broke. We know how it was used and ours don't break like this from the way we know it was used. No doubt about that. I'm confident it's not stainless steel, but I'm having the metallurgy done as we speak. I should have those results for you tomorrow along with its tensile strength. That means its breaking point, if you don't know."

"I do know. My father is a farrier, and that means he fits metal horseshoes, if you don't know."

"Touché," the doctor said. "I should have given you more credit. Sorry, no offense intended."

"None taken," Spencer said. "This has been enormously helpful, and I really appreciate the time you have given this. I'm not sure where this will take me, but it's a lot more than what I started with this morning."

After the call with Dr. Redmond, Spencer was excited to share the results with Butler. The Middle East connection gave him pause. Was this just a body parts case or a kidnapping for some other purpose? He wanted to share his analysis with his seasoned former detective.

"Amy, please find Butler and ask him to come see me ASAP."

It wasn't long before Butler arrived. "Any developments worth talking about?" he asked.

"I just got off the phone with Dr. Redmond about that broken blade. He hasn't had time to do the metallurgy, but he recognized the blade as not coming from a U.S. manufacturer

108

or the British one that is the usual source of scalpels."

"Okay, so how does that help?" Butler asked. "What's the big deal?"

"The big deal is that he recognized its shape and apparent composition as coming from the Middle East. Maybe Syria, Iraq or even Iran."

"What makes him so sure?"

"I got a lesson on scalpels – origins and what not – and he has actually seen one like this, down to the broken blade. That actually helped because theirs break, and ours don't. Considering his opinion, what do you make of it?"

"More importantly, what do you make of it?" Butler asked.

"I'm going to apply a little Sutton's Law here that I think makes sense."

"What's Sutton's Law? You're not talking about Willie Sutton, the bank robber?" Butler asked in disbelief that a crook could help.

"I am, and I had the exact thought when I first heard it. Let me walk you through it. Willie stole from banks because that's where the money is. Medical schools adopted his logic as a key method of coming to a diagnosis. That is, always start with the most obvious answer. It worked for Sutton until he was caught, and it works in the medical field. I learned it from Lisa. She said they actually teach it in med school. Why not apply it here, too? Here's what I think is obvious from all this. If the scalpel came from, say, Syria, it was being used by a Syrian. And if a Syrian is responsible, why would he or they come all the way to Rutledge just for a parts baby? He or they wouldn't, would they?"

"I like the logic, but there's not much supporting evidence, and there's a lot of what you guys call suppositions or assumptions. You know, though, the one thing that really bothers me about what Dr. Thomas said when he threw us out of his office was in response to you asking if the baby was still alive. We were on the body parts trail, and he said something along the line of he couldn't or wouldn't talk about that. Wouldn't he say, 'I don't have a clue?' if he didn't know?"

"My point exactly," Spencer said. "I was going to get to that – honest. Now what?"

"Are you going to give this to the feds?"

"Absolutely, but not until I get enough that means something, so I don't look like a rookie again. Besides, I told Rollins I would stay out of this, except for the murders, and so far, I can't prove any connection, even if I believe there is one. Dr. Redmond is still having the metal analysis done, and that might tell us more, but I don't know what, other than where it may have come from. That's intriguing, but that's about it."

"Not that it matters, but I think that's the right call."

"It always matters, or I wouldn't be asking. By the way, I'm meeting an ER nurse at Rutledge Hospital at 1:00. She said she was afraid for Mrs. Simpson being brought out of her coma and wants to talk to me. I don't know any more than that, but maybe she's worried about practices and procedures in the ER or something else. I talked to Manning, and she heard Mrs. Simpson was successfully brought out this morning and didn't remember anything concrete, except she remembered her baby crying."

"Was it a boy or a girl?"

"Manning didn't say. I am assuming she would have told me, if she heard."

After that meeting concluded, Spencer had just enough time to crack and jam down two hard boiled eggs that were his lunch of choice when he was on a tight schedule. As a kid, hanging around the many farms his father worked in the farrier trade, he ate a lot of eggs for lunch that gave him just enough to get through the day before his usual dinner recipe – four and a half minutes on high and no need to peel back the cover.

For Spencer, life was a contradiction between sheer excitement and pure boredom. Kayleigh would change all that, he hoped.

Chapter Twelve

Spencer worked his way through the noon hour traffic on his way to Rutledge Hospital. It occurred to him that the scheduled interview resulted from a failure to delegate. He considered the fact that he jammed down his lunch because he wouldn't let any of his stable of attorneys or staff take charge. Once again, he knew that failure came from his father, who lived by a variation of the Golden Rule: Never ask anyone to do anything you wouldn't do yourself and then do it yourself, if at all possible. Delegation, Spencer realized, would always be a problem.

As he came up to the last traffic light before the hospital, he could not help looking to the car stopped at his left. Sure enough, the driver was texting and would remain there long after Spencer pressed on. Texting was an epidemic of an uncontrollable habit, and one that gave him the answer to the missing phone of Alice Simpson at the doctor's office. That was the only answer he had, and Sutton's Law, so far, was of little use. Nothing was breaking his way.

Spencer walked into the main floor of the hospital, and immediately a familiar voice called out to him. "Spencer Tallbridge, what brings you here?" It was Agent Rollins with a cadre of fellow agents, no doubt at the hospital to see Mrs. Simpson.

"Hello, Rollins. I'm just here to see a friend, but I heard already that Mrs. Simpson was brought back successfully. Also heard she couldn't remember anything helpful."

"You've got good sources!"

"It's the coroner. Remember, she's a doctor, and she knows a lot of people here. Was she right?"

"She got it right. We came up with nothing, but we didn't press. We were told by a physician that pressing now is not a good idea. He called it traumatic amnesia, and there's not a very good prognosis for her ever getting her memory back. We're just going to give her time and hope for the best, but it's not promising. Anything going on with the murders?"

"We're empty too. You probably know the ambulance had nothing of evidentiary value, and canvassing also came up with nothing. No witnesses. Thomas had to know his killer. The receptionist left that day and locked the door behind her leaving the doctor and nurse to do end-of-day paperwork. I figure Thomas let his killer in, but who knows? There was no DNA on the door handle. It was wiped clean. That's about all I know, except speculation on the number of killers it took to do the injections. The sheriff is also following up on locating any cell phones belonging to the doctor, nurse or Mrs. Simpson, but no word on that yet. Are you still following the ransom possibility, or are you convinced it was for body parts?" Spencer asked.

"We're working both, but there is very little to work with. I was hoping our intel would have something by now. Maybe some confirmation or an explanation, but nothing." 'Hoping for intel' was polite 'FBI speak' for a snitch, and Spencer did not have one either. He thought about teasing Rollins with the Middle East hypothesis about the scalpel, but that was still a rabbit hole he wasn't supposed to be going down, and he had nothing to support it. "Better left unsaid for now," he thought.

After Rollins and his fellow agents left for the parking lot, Spencer walked over to the information desk.

"I'm Spencer Tallbridge, and I'm here to meet someone. Has anyone asked for me?"

Spencer was on time, and the area was not very crowded. In a business suit and tie, his presence would be obvious to anyone looking for him.

"No, sir, I have been here for about a half hour. I came on duty at 12:30, and no one has asked for you. I'm sure of that. Can you tell me who you're looking for? Is it a hospital employee, perhaps a doctor?"

"No, Just a friend. I'll give her a call in a few minutes just to see what's holding her up."

Spencer found a bench nearby and waited. His wait went from minutes to tens of minutes, and finally, he decided to call her. That part of that plan had not been planned well. He had not brought the message with her number that Amy gave him the day before. He could count on Amy to have it and made a call.

"Hello, Amy. I'm still at Rutledge, and that Rowland lady is a no show. I need to call her to see if I should wait, but I forgot to bring her number. Can you bring it up?

"You forgot something? That's not like you."

"Careful," Spencer said, letting out a small degree of frustration with being stood up.

Amy supplied the number, and Spencer made the call.

"Hello, Teresa Rowland? This is Spencer Tallbridge, and I'm at the information desk."

"I'm sorry. I don't need to talk to you now. I should have called. I'm really sorry. I just can't talk to you now. I hope you will understand. Goodbye."

She gave Spencer no time to convince her otherwise and hung up. It was just another dead end. Spencer did not move to leave. He simply sat where he was to trying to make sense of Teresa's change of direction. Teresa called because she was afraid for Alice Simpson. She wanted to talk to Spencer before Alice was brought back from the coma, but now that Alice was back, with no significant memory of the assault, Teresa wants to clam up, he considered. Moreover, it was reported in the hospital record that when Alice first arrived at the hospital, she awakened briefly, but said nothing. So what is Teresa afraid of? Spencer questioned. He needed, at least, to find out why he was so rudely stood up and what she wanted to say at first. It was time for one more call to get to the bottom of this.

"Hello, Doc," Spencer said to Dr. Manning. "I'm calling for a favor. Would you check the admission hospital record and tell me which nurses were working in the ER when Alice Simpson was brought in? More importantly, I need to know which nurse made the record that said Mrs. Simpson first woke up and had no memory before her coma was induced. I don't think I'm asking for anything I'm not permitted to get."

"Maybe, but I think you should have it. If I get that for you, you can't disclose where you got it. I don't need to be brought into that kind of records issue with the hospital. Are you going to tell me why or what you're looking for?"

"Honestly, it's just a hunch. A nurse from the ER called with something she wanted to tell me before Alice Simpson was brought out of her coma, and now she stood me up."

"Ah, a jilted lover!"

"I have been a jilted lover, but not by her!" Spencer said with a laugh and thinking of a long past relationship that ended badly for him. His laugh acknowledged that they both still retained a sense of humor. "Give me a break. And really, just give me the names, okay?"

"You'll have them by the end of the day, and thanks for putting up with my jokes."

"You're the best, Doc. I'll keep it to myself, I promise," Spencer said, and he left the hospital. There was a temptation to stop at Alibis and see Kayleigh, but he would have to put that off for now. He was waiting on the names of the ER nurses, and he felt like he was now waiting for a jury verdict. The thought of what may be in the hospital record, or not in the record, began to consume him just like considering what a jury might be doing during their deliberations. It was the only lead he had, and just as he had told Lisa, it was really nothing more than a hunch.

When Spencer arrived back at his office, he asked Amy to get Arnold. As his chief of the felony division, Spencer needed one of Arnold's 'full reports', as Arnold called them, concerning operations.

"Arnold, I have to tell you I have been a little distracted lately with the Thomas murders. I feel that I haven't kept my finger on the pulse around here. Anything I should know?"

"Well, Boss," Arnold began, "I'd say the office is running like a well-oiled machine, except for that hiccup in the Simpson kidnapping case. I think you're out of the woods on that one, and there's nothing problematic working. You haven't missed anything, if that's what you're asking."

"That's exactly what I'm asking. It's funny how nervous I get when I'm out of contact. Maybe because I really am new at this prosecution gig."

"We think you're doing fine, sir, and no one's complaining," Arnold concluded.

Spencer and Arnold talked for another hour, scheduling other cases and assignments before Amy interrupted the meeting to tell Spencer that the coroner was on the phone.

"Hello, Doc. Were you able to get the names?"

"Sure did. Are you ready to write?"

"Go ahead."

"There were three nurses that were looking after her at first. Their names are Becky Fulton, Teresa Rowland and Sylvia Dirks. The one who wrote the note in the record about Alice Simpson regaining consciousness briefly was...." The coroner was interrupted by Spencer with a question and an answer.

"Can I guess? It was Teresa Rowland, right?"

"Good guess. What are you up to, Spencer? What's going on?"

"Maybe something and probably nothing, but I'll let you know."

"If there's a problem with hospital staff over there, I need to know, or the hospital needs to know."

"I'm not there yet, but I'll let you know. Until then, keep this to yourself, okay?"

"Sounds like you're playing detective again. Is that right?" she asked.

"Let's just call it collateral interest, but please keep it to yourself for now."

"I will. I just don't want you to get ground into that quick you're always trying to avoid."

"Warning noted and thanks," Spencer said. He ended the call and again called out to Amy.

"Amy, Butler now, please."

"On the phone or here?" she asked.

"Here, please, and see if you can get an address for that Teresa Rowland on the reverse phone index."

It was not long before Butler arrived, and Amy had an address. Spencer explained to Butler what he learned about Teresa Rowland and his interest in talking to her that day. He did not like being stood up, but his interest went way beyond something personal. She was the only lead he had in both cases – Simpson and Thomas.

"I would like you to come along," Spencer said.

"I'm fine with that, Boss, but I would like you to consider what happened the last time we jumped a possible witness. I don't think you will withstand another suicide claim, all things considered."

"You mean like promising Rollins I'm staying out of the Simpson case?"

"Exactly," Butler said.

"Point well taken. I figure she's on a day rotation, so she should be home after seven, and that's when I'll drop by just to clear the air about being stood up. That should be a safe pretext."

"I'll run a LEADS check on her and verify her address. I'll also check what car she drives; if it's at her home, there's a good bet she will be there. Try to be nice."

"Good detective work, my friend, and I will."

"I figure she'll be home by six," Butler offered, "so I'll just swing by and take a look. I'll give you a call, if I see the car."

"Okay. Thanks, but I intend to stop anyway. Who knows? Maybe she carpools or her car's out of sight in her garage. I want to get to the bottom of this today. I'll look for your call."

"If you don't mind, would you call me with whatever you find out?" Butler asked.

"Count on it," Spencer said.

Chapter Thirteen

Spencer stayed at his office until 6:30 P.M. when Butler called with his observations as planned. Her car was in the driveway, along with her husband's, so Spencer could expect meeting more than just her. There would not be an angry dog to add to the mix, he hoped.

On arrival, he announced his presence by ringing the doorbell, with no result. Straining to hear, there was nothing to indicate it was working, so a good knock on the door was his last option with a desired result.

As the door opened, a medium-sized man with a crew cut asked directly, "And you want to talk to my wife, right?"

"I do," Spencer said, at first without introduction. "It's important she talks with me. I take it you know who I am?"

"You're the Prosecutor, Spencer Tollbridge," he said firmly, "and she doesn't want to talk to you."

Spencer could not hold back a laugh at the mispronunciation of his name. The last time it happened was when he was called Tollbridge by a judge, and he had to correct him that there was no toll to it. The same would be done now, and perhaps break the ice that was quickly forming.

"It's Tallbridge, no toll to it, and I'm here to help. If your wife won't talk to me, at least let me talk to you so you know what this is all about. It won't take long." Spencer avoided anything threatening, and his offering of prosecutorial help to lift the burden that must be bothering Teresa and her husband was bait that could not be refused.

"Okay. Come on in. What's this all about?"

"I don't know how much you know about the lady whose baby was kidnapped, but I know your wife may have valuable information. I know she was concerned for that woman's safety, and I need to talk to her."

Spencer reached into his coat pocket and pulled out a folded receipt for a chair he bought as a phony subpoena.

"I have a subpoena that I don't want to use. I don't want anyone to ever know we talked. I can do that, and I will do that. But if she will not talk to me, I'll just leave, but leave this subpoena for her to appear at a grand jury hearing. I don't want that. I don't want the hospital to ever know we talked, but if she's subpoenaed, I can't help it getting out. Are you getting this?"

Just as Teresa's husband was about to defend his wife further, she came around the corner from another room. She was tearful, but not crying and her eyes were bloodshot. She sat down on a chair and just looked at Spencer as if to size him up for what was to follow.

"Hello, Teresa," Spencer began. "I know you're afraid. You told me that in your first call, but now that apparently changed after Mrs. Simpson was brought out of her coma. I need to know why."

"I wanted to talk to you," Teresa began. "I wanted to tell you. I changed her record. I couldn't live with myself. I know I'll get fired for what I did. I know it. But later when she came out of it and couldn't remember anything, I thought I could just pretend it didn't happen," she said at a record pace.

"You have said a lot, but I just need you to slow down. To put your mind at ease, let me make a deal with you. Whatever you tell me tonight, will never be told to the hospital or anyone else that could ever tell. That is my promise to you, and your husband is a witness to this. It just needs to be the truth – deal?"

"Deal," she said, and her husband nodded in agreement.

"Take me through it, soup to nuts, from the first time you saw Mrs. Simpson. Don't worry, I don't have a recorder going, if either of you are wondering about that. I just need the whole story."

"My name is Doug, Mr. Tallbridge. I do believe you, and I think Teresa does, too. Teresa has been going through hell with this. It took her a long time just to tell me what happened. She's a good person and a good nurse. It means everything to her and just the thought of getting fired...." He could not complete his thought, but it was obvious to Spencer, who finished it for him.

"It would ruin your lives, wouldn't it?"

"It would. We are simple people. We both work. Teresa saves people every day, and now this problem for something she thought was right, and I think she still feels it was the right thing to do. If it got out that she changed a hospital record, she would never be able to work in a hospital again. Do you understand?"

"I do," Spencer said, "but tell me, why did you pick me as the first person to be told?" Spencer asked, directing the question to Teresa.

"When this all happened, I wasn't going to tell anyone, but when I thought she might remember what happened to her when she came out of the coma, I knew I had to tell someone, or she might be killed. I remembered all the stories about how you saved Mr. McBride, and I just felt you would understand. When she couldn't remember anything, I felt I was off the hook, so to speak, and didn't have to say anything. Somehow, I guess I said too much without thinking, and you put it together."

"Thanks. That warms my heart, really. Now what happened?"

"I was working an afternoon shift in the ER. It was from 2:00 to 10:00. We weren't very busy that day. A guy came in with a typical chain saw injury to his leg and needed a dozen or so stitches. There was another guy that had an episode of syncope – that means he was passing out at home, and his wife brought him in for an assessment. Really, just a routine afternoon until we got a call to expect Mrs. Simpson. We didn't know her name then, but we knew she was coming and in real trouble. When she arrived, we took her right into a treating unit, and all the equipment was ready. We had a portable X-ray machine, and we hooked her up to the standard stuff. You know- respiration, oxygen saturation, temperature, blood pressure and an EKG. We knew how serious it was. I heard she had been stabbed in the chest, and a broken scalpel blade was recovered. Her placenta was still in place, and there was a fear of septicemia, a pulmonary embolism, and anything else

119

that didn't belong there."

"I've heard the coroner mention those medical problems in other cases, but I never needed to ask what they are. Can you help me with those?" Spencer asked.

"Sure. Septicemia is a bacterial blood infection, and it can cause toxic shock that is deadly. We heard Mrs. Simpson was attacked in the back of a squad, and obviously that's not a very sterile place for a major surgery with so many bugs and germs around. A pulmonary embolism, in simple language, is a blood clot that goes to the lungs, and it can also kill you by blocking oxygen transport. We usually see PEs in fairly bloody procedures, like total hip replacements, but in recent years we are taught to look for them in C-Sections like this one, and obviously it was bloody as hell. Does that help?"

"Very much. Thank you. What happened next?"

"She already was receiving fluids when she arrived, but we checked that just the same and drew blood for testing. Her vitals were pretty good considering what she had gone through. Her wrists had been cut and repaired. I did a peripheral blood check by squeezing her index fingernail. It's called a capillary refilling test. When I released pressure, her nail bed pinked up almost immediately from a pale color telling me she had good circulation to her finger from the repair of the laceration of her radial artery in her wrist. I checked the other hand, and it was the same. The blood came back from the lab, and her hemoglobin and hematocrit were on the low side as well as platelets that were also low. Those first two are a measure of how well her blood was transporting oxygen, and the platelets are important for coagulation. She was literally a bloody mess when she came in, and the doctor ordered whole blood. That would resupply those as long as she didn't have an embolism. My job was also to make sure everything got in the record, and that is where I got myself in trouble."

"You're not in trouble. It really is amazing what you do that you think is just routine. You can be my ER nurse anytime," Spencer said with honest gratitude in his voice.

"Well, after we got her stabilized," she continued, "and the doctors closed the Cesarean and reworked her chest wound, the doctors left to work on an accident case and planned to return to put her in an induced coma even though she was still unconscious. I was alone with her just monitoring, and that's when it happened."

"When what happened?" Spencer asked.

"She woke up calling for Carl, who we later learned was her husband. I couldn't stop her from talking, and a lot of it didn't make any sense. She said they stole her baby boy. She said she saw it was a boy, and he was crying after the guy slapped his buttocks. They also said it had to be a boy, or they were going to kill someone. They were going to be riding a reptile for money. It didn't make sense. It just didn't make any sense," Teresa said hurrying with her conclusion.

"I need you to slow down. I get that it didn't make any sense, because it doesn't make any sense to me either, if I heard you correctly, and something about riding a reptile for money," Spencer said.

"That's exactly what she did say. She said one of the attackers had a scar down to his mask and black eyes. Her exact words. I'm not sure what she meant by black eyes. Maybe from a fight like we see here with the late-night drunk crowd or maybe just black-colored eyes. I don't know. There was a woman, too, she said, and she acted like a nurse. She also said they were all foreigners, maybe three of them, and then she passed out again. I thought it was crazy talk, a delirium in our world, and I was about to call for a doctor when one walked into the room. I was standing in the shadows of a corner, and I don't think he saw me at first, and then he seemed startled. I was just about to tell him what she said about identifying whoever did this to her when I noticed his name tag, and then his eyes, that I didn't notice at first. I guess I was distracted by his mask, and I really didn't think anything was wrong. It's the type of mask we all wear in the ER around people with open wounds like the ones Mrs. Simpson came in with, so no big deal. It's sort of like in a burn unit where we are very concerned about infection. Then I saw his name tag, and it said Dr. Richard Goodman. I've known him for years, and he doesn't have a foreign accent like this guy. Dr. Goodman was also in New York on vacation with his wife. Then there were his eyes. They were black even in the light, and then I saw his medical coat pocket where his tag was. He had a broken scalpel in it blade up. I could see the break to it, and it all came together. I got scared, real scared. He asked me how she was doing and if she regained consciousness. Those would ordinarily be normal questions, but then he wanted to know if she remembered anything. I lied and said she did wake up, but couldn't remember anything before she passed out again. With that, he left. Maybe I watch too much TV and movies, but I thought he was there to kill her. I could have told him she never woke up, but I wanted him to know she woke up and had no memory, otherwise he might come back. I thought I was being smart. Now, not so much. I don't know if this could have helped catch that guy or anyone else, but I was scared, and I still am. Can you understand? I falsified the record, and said she woke up and couldn't remember anything. It was such an easy decision to help her, and now I have to live with it. Half of what I said was true. She did wake up, but the other half was a lie."

"There are times when it takes doing something wrong for the right thing to happen and in my opinion, this is one of those," Spencer said, offering prosecutorial absolution.

"I didn't know if that guy would be back. I worked doubles to watch her after that, and I made sure someone was with her when I was gone, and that was not for very long. If she got killed, I knew it would be my fault. When I heard she was about to be brought back, well, you know the rest. Can you forgive me for this? I'm not a criminal. Really, I'm not," she said tearfully.

"Of course, you're not. Like I said, you can be my ER nurse anytime. Okay?"

"I didn't know at first why she was working so much, and then she told me. I want you to know that no matter what happens, I'm proud of her," her husband said.

"Nothing is going to happen," Spencer promised. "This conversation never happened, but I can't tell you how grateful I am. I can't tell you what will happen next, but finally we can put together what probably happened beyond just speculation. How could you tell it was a broken scalpel?"

"There was a stem that narrowed to the broken part. The stem part was down in his shirt pocket, and where the blade was broken off, it was exposed. It wasn't like a shiny bread knife or a jack knife. In my mind, if you extended the broken part, it's a scalpel. Maybe, because I see the blades all the time, I knew it was a scalpel with a broken blade. Can you see what I'm saying?"

"I know exactly what you're describing."

"Do you think her baby is still alive?" Teresa asked.

"I know you will never discuss this, but yes, I do, and God willing, and the creek don't rise, we will find her boy." Spencer loved that old country worn out cliché. He knew people always thought he was referring to rising water, the way Johnny Cash sang it, when in fact it was about uprisings of Creek Indians in the early days of the Old South.

After thanking the Rowlands for letting him into their home and lives, he warned them not to disclose a word of what just took place. His confidentiality could only be guaranteed if she and her husband stuck to her original story. They both understood and were relieved that their burden had finally been lifted by the highest legal authority in the county. Teresa's last words to Spencer were, "If we can't trust you, who can we trust?" and he remembered those words spoken in the McBride case with a good result. If there were any truth in Spencer's Law, he thought, he would go two for two.

Chapter Fourteen

Spencer only drove a couple of blocks out of sight of the Rowland's to call Butler with the new development. Butler's confidentiality was assured, and Spencer felt no hesitation in telling Butler the news in spite of his promise to the Rowlands.

"Butler, it's Spencer."

"And I'm not supposed to recognize your voice, Boss?"

"Have I got a story for you, and it puts it all together just about like we figured. I just finished up with nurse Rowland. Do you want the short version or the whole story?"

"The short version. It's not that I'm not interested or busy. I am actually real interested and would like to get to the point, if it's all the same to you."

Without a preface or preamble, Spencer unpacked her story. "Teresa Rowland was the duty nurse when Mrs. Simpson came in. She worked with the doctors on the medical issues of Mrs. Simpson, and Teresa was eventually alone with her. Mrs. Simpson came to and said some crazy stuff but gave a description of two men and a woman. She said they were wearing those medical face masks, but she heard their voices, saw the eyes of one, and he had an unusual scar above his eye and black eyes. She was probably referring to their color, but that's just Rowland's opinion. Foreign accents are in this, too. Alice saw she had a baby boy, and the kidnappers apparently also wanted one. They would kill someone if it weren't. Mrs. Simpson then passed out again. Teresa was about to call the doctors when an imposter doctor came in and asked if she came to. She recognized he was a phony from his name tag, so she lied and said Mrs. Simpson came to, but couldn't remember anything. He had a broken scalpel in his shirt pocket. She then falsified the record that Mrs. Simpson couldn't remember anything to protect her, and I gave her a pass on all that."

"Good job, Spencer. I don't think you could have gotten all that with me there. What was the crazy stuff? Seems to me she was making pretty good sense on the descriptions."

"I agree, but it doesn't make sense, if Teresa got it right. Maybe she misunderstood. Simpson said a bad guy was going to be 'riding a reptile for money' and I don't know how riding a reptile gets you there. Simpson did say that she heard her baby cry after getting a good slap on his rear and saw that it was a boy. The bad guys wanted a boy."

"Good sign, Spencer. I mean about it having to be a boy. I think it's better than a tossup that the kid is still alive, but where the hell is he? The accent part scares the shit out of me, too."

"What makes you think the kid is still alive from what was said?" Spencer asked.

"You and I talked about this. If they want parts, going to all the trouble of attacking a pregnant woman who is eight months down the road to delivery, seems like a stretch. You might want to ask Lisa if using a premature baby boy for parts is at a premium in any medical field," Butler said.

"Good call. I'll do it tomorrow. Let's sleep on this tonight and talk in the morning. See ya."

On Spencer's way home he felt relieved that he was making progress. He was at a point where he could think of other things instead of what had become an obsession with the Simpson case. He passed by Dog by the Pound hoping to see lights on, but the shop was closed. It would have been a good diversion to see the animals, all friendly and looking for a home, he thought. He did want to hear the good news from the owner, Janet, about the McBrides and the Labrador puppy he bought them the night McBride was released, almost a year earlier.

FRIDAY

9: 00 A.M.

Chapter Fifteen

The next morning at the office, Spencer was ready to get back up to speed with his new information and wanted to talk with the coroner about Butler's question before reviewing the case with him. It was now the seventh day after the assault, and Spencer felt he was making progress in spite of the weekend beginning the next day to slow it down.

"Amy, would you get the coroner on the line, please?"

Spencer always had a way of making an order sound like a polite question, and with Amy, there was no misunderstanding or how to respond other than by calling Dr. Manning.

"Hello, Doc," Spencer began in his usual way. "I have a question in this Simpson case. Do you have a minute?"

"Sure, Spencer. What's on your mind?"

"We're trying to get a handle on whether the Simpson's baby is alive or in a parts box, like the FBI thinks. We've been kicking this around, and I have to agree with Butler that going after a pregnant woman, to us, doesn't make much sense, but maybe it does to you or some kind of medical specialist, if it's more than a kidnapping? Do you get our point?"

"Truthfully, I always wondered why those parts cases keep coming up. They do happen, but at one month before delivery? What remains then, I guess, is the ransom idea and maybe a better outcome. Is the FBI following the ransom motive?"

"It is, but I think the FBI's working theory is still some parts thing, because of past experience. Would it make any difference if the kidnappers were after a boy or girl baby?"

"Do you think that is what's going on?" Lisa asked.

Spencer had to lie. Given his commitment to Teresa Rowland, he could not share what he knew.

"No. We were just wondering, if that kind of thing would make any difference?"

"For parts, I don't think so. What's going on down the parts road usually has to do with stem cells and organs, and those are limited. I mean, in a baby, there's not that much useable, so it's usually the stem cells."

"I think you lost me," Spencer said, admitting his medical ignorance. "Can you go back to stem cells?"

"Well, this gets complicated. First, we all come from stem cells that are general cells that can become most any part of the body. Technically, they are called multipotent stem cells. The drill is getting them as soon as possible. Sex makes no difference. In the Simpson case, there would have been plenty of stem cells, right down to the umbilical cord, but that wasn't taken. It was just cut, left behind, and that was it. From pathology, I did see that the remaining length is what you would expect to find in any normal birth. Going after organs is another story, and again, sex won't make much, if any, difference. Say you're looking for a liver or liver tissue, a kidney or kidney tissue or even a heart valve, sex won't make any difference, even if you're in it for the Frankenstein Effect."

"What the hell is that?"

"We don't get to talk about that one much, but sometimes, and rarely from the reported cases. Living bodies are cut up and parts are regrown for research by countries not bound by our conventions. So, a baby, usually a fetus, is stolen, and its parts are grown essentially in a jar for use later, sort of like Frankenstein. I know that's an oversimplification, but I think you get the drift. Sex just doesn't usually play a role there, but it is always possible, I suppose. Using a baby at eight months is a little late for that approach."

"When the Simpson baby was stolen, would it be necessary to give the baby that old swat on the butt to kick start breathing, like we see in the movies to keep the baby alive?" Spencer wanted to know if there was any significance to how breathing was started. Why would the assailants care about respiration if the baby was just for parts? Mrs. Simpson said there was an effort to start the baby breathing with the rear end slap, and that may be important, Spencer thought, in determining if the baby were still alive.

"You're watching way too many movies and old ones at that. We don't slap anymore. We used to do that back in the fifties. You know, pick up the baby by the ankles and give it a swat, but not here anymore. Babies will start breathing just by being rubbed without the slap."

"What do you mean 'not here anymore'?" Spencer asked.

"That's interesting. We stopped the slap thing, but in the Middle East, like in Pakistan, they still do it. I never asked why. It's probably some cultural thing, but I don't know. What's always bothered me in the Simpson case is the medical professionalism of the kidnappers, or at least the surgeon, to take the baby. Usually, in the cases I've seen or read about, the attacker is some loon, usually a female, who wants a baby and thinks getting one is as simple as popping a big pimple. Cut, pop and out comes the baby, and often the baby and mother end up dead. It's real butchery, and in this case, I have to tell you, the surgeon, doctor or not, knew what he or she was doing. All things being said, it could be either, parts or a live baby, but I'm betting on a live baby somewhere even though death usually has a way of finding me. There is one thing you need to know, and I might not be the best source of opinion, but at eight months gestation, that baby is premature and might need help. Maybe even hospital help. You might want to talk to someone about that."

"Thanks, Lisa. This has been very helpful, and I agree with your assessment just by putting what we have together. You know that's where I live, and your medical assessment helps to keep me out of the weeds. Any suggestions on an obstetrician?"

"You're welcome. Happy to help, and you might want to call Dr. Melvin Davis. I don't have his number handy, but he's in Henderson. Tell him I asked you to call."

Spencer now had an even better picture of what probably happened than he had when he started that morning, and he was anxious to talk to Butler to hear any overnight insight he may have acquired.

"Amy, please find Butler and ask him to come in."

"He's here already and coming down the hall," she said. Moments later, Butler arrived and got right to the point. "Morning, Boss. Did you have a chance to talk with the coroner?"

"Yes, and let me boil it down for you. First, she thinks the baby is alive and isn't convinced it's a parts case. It could be but keeping the ransom motive going is a better bet. She thinks it makes more sense that the kidnappers are after a live baby to keep alive. Now here's the showstopper. She says the butt slap to start the baby breathing hasn't been done here since the fifties. It's a Middle East thing, and she used Pakistan as an example. She gave me a lot of medical stuff on why the parts theory is not likely, and on your question, the sex wouldn't make any difference, if it was just taken for parts."

"Okay, so where do we go from here?" Butler asked.

"I was hoping you could tell me after sleeping on it."

"Sorry. I'm at a loss too, but if they have the baby, and it's going to the Middle East, don't you think you should tell the feds about this?"

"Ordinarily, I would agree with you, but I promised Teresa and her husband that I wouldn't, and if that baby is going the Middle East or is already there, there's nothing we or they can do about it. I know that sounds like a rationalization, but how would anyone start looking for a baby when the only thing we know is that it's a boy. She did say one thing, however, that I need to check. She seems to think that at eight months gestation, there might be a medical problem with the baby, so we need to check with an obstetrician, and she gave me a name."

"I think that's important, if there is any chance the baby can't be moved out of the country now. But I still I don't know where to start. Do you want me to make that call?"

"No. I think I know what to ask. I'll give him a call. Amy, would you come in, please?"

Amy came in and brought her note pad. His question usually meant more than just getting someone on the line, and she was prepared as usual.

"Amy, I want you to get the number of Dr. Melvin Davis over in Henderson and find out when it would be a good time for me to call him with a question about premature babies. Tell him, or his secretary, that Dr. Manning gave him as a reference."

"If he's in, do you want me to put him through?"

"Absolutely," Spencer concluded. With that, Amy returned to her desk.

"So, what now?" Butler asked.

130

"I don't know. We've got a lot of clues, but what good are they? I think we can conclude that the kidnappers wanted an unborn male baby and that they are probably from the Middle East. One has a vertical scar above his eye and probably really black eyes, and one is a female. There was a third with no description, and he may have been the driver and perhaps one more. Add in the pick-up driver seen by Walcott, that makes a team of four or five."

"And they wanted a boy, right?"

"Right, but why?"

"Didn't Mrs. Simpson tell Teresa Rowland they were in it for money?"

"Yes, and riding a reptile, if that makes any sense."

"Not to me," Butler said. "And they wanted to kill Mrs. Simpson, too."

"Also, right. That doesn't give us enough to buy a cup of coffee."

"I have Dr. Davis on the line," Amy announced.

"I'll take it, thanks. Put him through."

"Hello, Dr. Davis. I'm Spencer Tallbridge, the Rutledge County Prosecutor. The coroner, Dr. Manning, said you might not mind answering a few technical questions about a premature birth, if you have time."

"I have the time. What's on your mind?"

"I'll do my best to explain it, but I need to know what medical problems a baby might have if born at eight months instead of the usual nine months."

"We would say the baby was just born a month early, and we call that preterm or a preemie," the doctor began to explain. "At just one month early, that is what we would consider borderline for neonatal care in the intensive care unit. Most all hospitals have those, if they are delivering babies. Is this a case where there was no unit, and something went wrong?"

"No, but I do want you to consider it's a Cesarean birth at eight months."

"Who's doing a Cesarean a month early around here? What was the emergency? Was it a car crash or a fall, because there's not much else that would explain that unless the mother is dead or dying? She wasn't dead or dying, was she?"

"No, and I would appreciate it, if you would keep this conversation just between us, okay?"

"Fine, but what happened? Is this that kidnapping case all over the news?"

"It is," Spencer said. "What I need to know is what are the complications for a baby at that age?"

"Respiration and nutrition, to name the most important ones on our differential, but there can be others that land a baby in the NICU. The baby isn't in the ICU, is it?"

"Not that I know of, but that's a good question and one I'll work on. I didn't realize a preemie at eight months would need that much intensive care. How long does a preemie spend in intensive care?"

"Sorry. I left my crystal ball at home. Really, there is no way to tell without knowing more, but there is a statistic. We did a study for insurance considerations and found that statistically there is a one-to-three relationship. That is, for every week premature, there will be three days spent in the NICU. So, if a baby is born four weeks premature, one month, you can expect twelve days in the NICU. Remember, though, that's just based on math and a large volume of cases. Could be a day or two either way. One kid could spend fifty days in the NICU having been just one week preterm. It's just a statistical analysis."

"Just the same, it gives me a window to work with and a date in five days when the window might be closing. How does a premature birth affect mental development?"

"That's interesting. Mark Twain was a preemie, and so was Sidney Poitier, the actor. The most amazing one is Albert Einstein, so I don't think there is a developmental issue with mentation, and maybe it's an asset. Maybe, if you want a really smart kid, pray for a preemie," Dr. Davis said in jest.

"My investigator is with me, and I just need to check something with him. Butler, is there anything I missed?"

"Ask him about the butt slap," Butler added.

"One more thing, doctor, if you don't mind. Is it really the case that you don't slap a baby on the buttocks to start them breathing? Dr. Manning said that's an outdated procedure, but she said they still do it overseas," Spencer asked, looking for corroboration from an obstetric expert.

"She's right, and I'm actually the one who told her that. And it's still done that way in the Middle East."

"Do you know why?" Spencer asked.

"I'm not really sure, but I think it has more to do with male dominance by doctors there. It lets everyone know who's in charge – men, all men – and the result is still the same. The breathing reflex is baked into our genes, and just a little rubbing with a towel when cleaning up gets things started. Does that help?"

"Too soon to tell, but I think so," Spencer answered. "I really appreciate your time."

"I'd start checking around to see if any neonatal intensive care unit took in a preemie lately, if I were you. You'll want to check the ER admissions, and that's the place to start."

"Count on it," Spencer said ending the call.

Chapter Sixteen

Following the call with Dr. Davis, Spencer and Butler both agreed that they finally had something to follow up in a case with no end in sight after they discussed the relevant information Dr. Davis provided.

"Man, I didn't know where to start until now, and I'll get on every baby ICU in a fifty-mile radius. I may as well go date-of-incident to now, don't you think?" Butler asked.

"No harm in that, and Davis said you'll want to start with the ER admissions. I think he's saying that if the baby came in for anything, it would come through an ER first. If the baby did end up in an ICU, we'd have twelve days from that, and that's based on statistics, but could be more or less. I'm going with twelve."

"Got it. I expect I'll be on the phone all day on this, and I'll keep in touch."

"I'll know what it is like to be an expectant father waiting for your call. Wouldn't it be great if we get a hit on this? I'll be a nervous wreck by the end of the day," Spencer said.

"Here's a suggestion. Alibis has a good bowl of bean soup and a shredded beef on special today. Why don't you just go over there and wait it out. The guys tell me you've been sniffing around Finnegan's daughter anyway, and she might take your mind off of this."

"I didn't know it was that obvious. I really just met her."

"They said you looked like you were hit by a Howitzer when you met her."

"Like I said, I didn't know it was that obvious. It's a good idea, and a good place to wait it out. Anyway, I've got another errand to run before that, so I should be there by noon. I'll look for your call."

Spencer needed a distraction and decided to start with a visit to Dog by the Pound. Janet, its owner, was always interesting with her advocacy for animal rights and had a good ear for what the locals were saying about how well Spencer was protecting dogs and cats. He found it amazing how much public interest there is for animal welfare. He could have a case with six abused children under the age of ten, held in a cage with no food or water by their parents, and the story would hardly make the evening news. It was just the opposite with dogs and cats. Do the same, and there would be protesters out to the street with signs, banners, and songs demanding the prosecution and a public hanging. Spencer did not mind, and he was fully aware that animal advocacy was cheap politics with an indictment and a little time as his only investments.

When Spencer arrived at Janet's pet shop, she was busy preparing the noon meals for all the livestock that were seeking attention. Her Labrador, Harriet, was the first to greet Spencer, and over the past year, she had gotten to know him well and by smell.

"Hello, Harriet," Spencer said, as Harriet hurried over to him with tail wagging and with a perceptible smile that he always maintained she had, but that no one else ever saw. "Are you a good girl?" and of course, she was. "Good morning, Janet. I got your message about something with the McBrides," he said questioningly.

"They're fine, but I want to tell you about their new adventure. Billy and Molly are moving out of their old place to a place in the country. Billy really loves Quick, and with the money he got from the State on the insurance settlement, he's going to start a dog kennel and training operation. I think it's great."

Billy received a substantial settlement based on his wrongful conviction and still had other claims pending to be determined after Herald's trial later that year. It was a good start. His dog, Quick, named after a favorite admonition of Spencer of a place never to grind into, helped him get back to a life of normalcy that may not have been possible without his animal friend.

"That's wonderful. No more stairs for Molly, and I think country life will agree with both of them. I don't see much of Molly anymore. She does drop by, but no longer to cuss me out.

135

I think my staff likes that part more than my saving her son's life," Spencer said with a laugh joined in by Janet.

"Are there any developments on that stolen baby case?" Janet asked.

"Nothing I can talk about. The FBI has it now, and the agents are working every angle."

"I read where you got involved with her doctor, and it didn't go well."

"No, it went about as bad as it could, but his death and the death of his nurse weren't my fault. Did you read that, too?"

"It was covered that way eventually. Funny how the press is slow to say anything good about anyone, except in the obits. Did Mrs. Simpson ever get to see her baby?"

"I can't say one way or the other. That's the way investigations are, but you can always hope she saw her baby and heard it cry."

"Too bad she's not a penguin looking for her chick."

"What's a penguin got to do with it?"

"Oh, I was just thinking about a nature program I saw about penguins in Antarctica, and the ability of a mother penguin to find her crying chick after her long return from the sea with food. She hears the chick among thousands and can tell it's hers."

"Nice daydream. Wish it was that easy. Unfortunately, I don't think we humans are wired up like penguins. What are you getting ready to feed there?" Spencer asked to change the subject.

"These are what we call meal worms, and I feed them to the turtles."

"How many do the little amphibians eat for lunch?" Spencer asked, trying to seem interested in the maggoty looking worms and well informed about the species before leaving for his own lunch.

"They're not amphibians. Turtles are reptiles. Frogs are amphibians," she said instructively."

Spencer suddenly felt like he really was hit by a Howitzer. He stood silent looking at his feet, and beyond deep thought.

"Don't take it so hard, Spencer. Most people don't know the difference between an amphibian and a reptile."

Spencer continued to stand motionless and silent.

"Is there something wrong? Did I say something wrong, Spencer?"

"You said everything right. I just can't explain it now, but I have to go."

Spencer was about to say more, but the light of inspiration hit him so hard he could not focus on a more coherent answer. He now saw the answer to the equation of the Simpson case that had been so elusive. The reptile was Rollins' boat, and Rollins was somehow a key player in the kidnapping, he thought. All the reasons for that came together in an instant, but he didn't have time to put them in order, but he knew he could, once he got back to Butler to sort it all out. Kayleigh, and the bowl of bean soup would have to wait.

***

Spencer wasted no time getting back to his office. It would be lunch time for most of his staff, but Butler would be working hard to contact area hospitals regarding any preemie admissions that might lead to the Simpson baby. On his return, Spencer went directly to Butler's office, where he was faithfully working on his assigned task. Spencer took a seat waiting for Butler's call to end.

"Any luck so far?" Spencer asked hopefully, trying hard to hold back his excitement about his solution of the Simpson case.

"Nothing yet, but I'm working the circle from the outside in," he said, without a more detailed explanation of his methodology. "What are you doing back? Kayleigh taking a day off?" Butler asked with a smirk.

"Who knows? I never made it over there, but I solved the whole damn Simpson case, and you're not going to believe it. Before you call me crazy, just hear me out. It's been so close and staring at us right in the face."

"Okay. What is it? The suspense is killing me," Butler said with doubt in his voice.

"It's Rollins. He's in on this. I don't know where to start, but he's in this up to his ass."

"Really? This ought to be good. Go ahead," Butler said.

"When I first met with Rollins," Spencer began, "he had a fish mounted on his wall and the picture of a turtle. They meant nothing to me, but I asked about them for small talk. He said they were to remind him of what he looked forward to in retirement not far off. The turtle reminds him of his boat, and he named his boat after it. He also said a turtle is an amphibian. Apparently, it's an old slow boat, and from what he said, I'm thinking he keeps it somewhere in Key West."

"I know you think there's a solution in that, but I'm not seeing it yet. So far, I see a pile of horseshit, and you're thinking there's a pony in there somewhere. I'm going to have a surprise here, right? There's a pony, right?" Butler questioned forcefully.

"You bet. When I went over to see Janet at Dog by the Pound before going to lunch, she was feeding a turtle, and I called it an amphibian. I really didn't know it's not an amphibian, but that's what Rollins called the one pictured on his wall – an amphibian. Janet corrected me and said it was a reptile, and then it hit me. Alice Simpson said one of her attackers would be riding a reptile for money. It has to be Rollins' boat. And he's in it for the money along with the rest."

Spencer paused for a moment, waiting eagerly for Butler's reaction and expecting the same excitement he experienced. Butler rocked back in his chair and said nothing. He just looked at Spencer with a look of disbelief.

Finally, Butler said, "You're making a joke, right? You're not really serious?"

"I am serious. It all fits. The kidnappers wanted a baby boy, right? We know, you and I, the baby is not for parts. Somebody wants a baby boy and is willing to pay a lot of money for it."

"So what? How does that get us – you – to Rollins?"

"The attackers are foreigners. We know that from their accents, and Rollins would be the perfect person to set it up. He has to have international connections."

"I haven't met many people in the medical profession lately that don't have an accent. Don't you think it's a stretch to conclude those guys are foreigners? You want to be accusing people of being foreigners just because of their accents? There go a few thousand votes," Butler opined.

"But what about the scalpel? It's probably from the Middle East."

"I have a butter knife at home, and who the hell knows where it came from. I'll bet you can get one on eBay that looks just like the broken blade we have and made out of the same stuff. You might want to consider that when you're trying to hang this on Rollins."

"I'm not trying to hang anything on anyone," Spencer said emphatically, defending the legitimacy of his conclusion.

"Well, you have to admit that you weren't too happy with Rollins when he asked you to keep out."

"But don't you see? That's exactly my point. He's perfect. I can't get involved. He shuts me out. It's supposed to be only a federal case, and when I did get in, I got hung out to dry by a guy about to retire and ready for a last big hit. In the FBI, retirement at 57 is mandatory, and he's pushing it."

"You did jump the gun with Dr. Thomas. I didn't ask you to do that. It was your call, not mine. So, let me see if I've got this straight. You meet with Rollins, and he tells you about his boat named after a turtle. He calls it an amphibian, and you find out it's actually a reptile. And the kidnappers know the difference. He's an FBI agent on the verge of retirement and thus has a motive to go big on a kidnapping and murder with Middle East types who are going for a ride on a reptile for money. Do you have any idea how stupid it sounds to accuse Rollins? Do you really think anyone would honestly consider your theory actionable, because honestly, I don't even consider it a theory? I can't support going after Rollins with this, and neither should you!"

"You sound like a guy trying to protect one of your own," Spencer said accusingly.

"What are you saying? You have a problem with me? I should have straightened you out when I first saw you."

"Saw me where?" Spencer asked.

"When you were breaking into the records center shortly after you got hired. Prescott heard from his sister that you were looking hard at the McBride case, and it got me thinking about you. I never met you but recognized you from around the courthouse. When I saw you that night walking alone in that neighborhood where the center is located, I followed you and saw you break in. I went in after you and was going to call you out but decided not to get involved with whatever you were doing in the dark. I knew I'd have to arrest you or make a report. Maybe you were just working overtime on some critical stuff. So, I cut you some slack and took a chance. Luckily for you it worked out."

"You were the person I saw down the street as I was leaving?"

"Yeah. When Herald went down, I thought we finally had someone special. Now I'm not so sure."

"Did it ever occur to you that if you stopped me, McBride would've been executed?"

"It did, but it probably doesn't matter to you what the hell, I think. That bothers me most of all. What I'm trying to tell you is that you are about to bite a big fat hog in the ass if you accuse Rollins with what you have. I've heard enough of this horseshit, and there's no pony here, but maybe a jackass. Take my advice and take a right or a left, but get off the Rollins' road, boat, turtle, or whatever you want to call it. I don't even want to hear about how you're planning to let this bullshit out of the bullshit bag. You're going to end up as the farm kid from Oklahoma who got lucky with the Herald case, blew it with Dr. Thomas and are about to self-destruct with Rollins and the entire FBI coming down on your head. I don't intend to watch, and in fact, I've had enough for one day. Unless you have a problem with me more than the insult, I'm outta here."

With that, Butler grabbed his coat and stormed out. Spencer realized that an order or request to stop and listen further would have been futile. For the first time, Spencer learned how close Butler had always been to him from the beginning and willing to act alone on his own conscience. Feeling deflated, he first thought about how he could have been more convincing. Obviously, he thought, he made a failed opening
140

statement to his only juror and was found wanting. Rollins, in Butler's mind, was acquitted. "What more could he have argued?" he asked himself. Maybe he should have given more emphasis to Rollins' upcoming retirement, which would give him a motive to kidnap the baby, but like everything else Butler argued, that was a stretch, too. Butler was a seasoned detective and probably knew better than he, Spencer thought, and in the final analysis, he had to conclude that he came up empty as far as proof was concerned with no hidden silver bullet looking to be found in the evidence he had.

When Spencer got back to his office, he did not hide his feelings well about his failed meeting with Butler. To Amy, his expression gave him away.

"What's going on?" Amy asked. "I'm not trying to interfere, but you look like a guy who just lost his best friend."

"I didn't know it showed," Spencer answered. "I may have, but I hope he will get over it."

"Who are you talking about, if you don't mind me asking?"

"It's Butler. I think I said something that pissed him off, if you don't mind that crude expression?"

"Maybe it fits. It's okay. I guess that explains him taking some time off," she said holding up a vacation time-off signature card.

"What's he taking?" Spencer asked.

"It doesn't say. It's open ended. You might have to work this out with him. Why don't you just give this a little time? I think you've been under the gun on that Simpson case, and maybe you both need a little time away from it and maybe each other," Amy suggested.

"You're probably right. I'm just waiting for something good to happen, and I thought I had it. I've waited long enough."

"You mean Spencer's Law? Your law that says that something good always happens if you wait long enough?"

"That and Sutton's Law. That's the one I was really thinking about."

"What's that one?"

"It simply means go with the simplest first, and that's what I thought I was doing, but I think Butler thinks it's just too simple or stupid. So much for laws, flaws and dead ends."

"I don't know what you're talking about, but I hope you and Butler can work it out," Amy said.

"Probably. I just need to give him time to cool off. He's a cop at heart and maybe a little more sensitive than I am. We'll see. Might be a good time to take a couple of hours away from this, too. Butler was working on a project, but I guess it can wait. I'll see you later. If I get any calls, just call me on my cell."

***

Spencer decided that a bowl of bean soup and the shredded beef might be a good idea after all, if Finnegan had any left, and seeing Kayleigh might just be what he needed to raise his spirits or provide a needed distraction from the funk he was falling into.

Spencer arrived at Alibis in mid-afternoon. The lunch crowd had left, and the after- work crowd had not arrived, giving Spencer an opportunity for Kayleigh's undivided attention.

"You're here early," Kayleigh observed with a welcoming smile.

"Just one of those days when I need to get away from it all."

"This might help," as she reached into the cooler to pull out a cold Bud.

"Hold off on that. I might get called out, and I don't want to smell like a brewery. I will take a bowl of Finnegan's bean soup though, if you have any left, and a shredded beef, too."

"I think I can arrange that," she said and called out the order through the kitchen door. "Everything okay in the prosecutor's office?" she asked generally.

"More or less," Spencer said, with a voice trailing off that implied much more and inviting another probing question from her.

"That doesn't sound good, Spencer. Something going on that you can talk about?"

As the daughter of a policeman, Kayleigh was aware of the limitations police and prosecutors had on discussing confidential information, and she knew better than to expect a detailed answer.

"Not really," Spencer responded. "Butler and I just had a disagreement, and it didn't go well. I'm waiting it out for a while," Spencer responded.

"You mean you're waiting to see who's going to blink first, right?"

"Very perceptive. I didn't look at it that way, but I think that's it."

"Can you tell me how it started?" Kayleigh asked.

"It was me, regrettably. I got all wound up with an idea about someone that needs prosecution or perhaps worse, and Butler didn't think too much of it."

"Tell Mr. Butler that I said that bad person should be eaten by a cat, and the devil should eat the cat! That's my wish for you."

"That's an odd expression. Never heard that one before," Spencer said, looking for an explanation.

"It's an old Irish saying we Irish use to deal with bad people. You probably say 'what goes around comes around' for giving bad people what they deserve."

"I think I insulted Butler somehow and that's how I see it."

"If you think that, you already know the 'somehow'," Kayleigh offered with further therapeutic bartender insight that was not lost on Spencer.

"Do you solve a lot of problems in your temporary line of work here?"

"Well, you know I'm going to law school, so a little practice is good, don't you think?"

"I guess that's why it also says 'Counselor-At-Law' on my license," Spencer said.

"I don't know what you got into with Butler, but do you want a little free advice?"

"Kayleigh, I'll take whatever you're serving up," Spencer said with a tone of exasperation.

"I know you're Butler's boss, and I know everyone sucks up to you because you're the prosecutor. I get all that, but you need to step back and get honest with yourself about what happened. You know the 'somehow' of what started this, and if you need to apologize, do it."

"Are you sure you're only 21?" Spencer asked after recognizing her insightful response.

"Bowl of bean soup and a shredded," Finnegan announced. "Hello, Tallbridge. You got the bottom of the barrel on the bean soup. Let me know if it's okay," as he put the tray in front of Spencer on the bar. "Getting a little therapy, are we, Spencer, my boy?"

"I would say you could call it that."

Finnegan leaned over close to Spencer's ear, but within range of Kayleigh, and said, "Just make sure it's not physical therapy," and went back into the kitchen with his point made.

The letter "a" was drawn out by Kayleigh as she yelled "Dad!" to note her displeasure with his interference with something that could become more personal. His message, though, was not lost on Spencer.

"So, what's it going to be?" Kayleigh asked.

"Be?" Spencer asked, wishing he could ask if physical therapy was in his future. That question was out of bounds by his standards.

"Are you going to call Butler and apologize?"

"I am, and after I finish your dad's finest, I will make the call."

It wasn't long before Spencer dialed Butler's phone, and it went immediately to voice mail.

"I think he's still pissed," Spencer said. "At least he knows I'm calling, and he'll call back."

Spencer and Kayleigh made small talk for another hour, but there was no call from Butler. Spencer called Butler's land line, and his wife told him that he was not home. She didn't know when to expect him back. It was Friday, and she said Butler was upset about something at work. He needed to get away and might not be back for a few days and possibly more.

It was not like Butler to leave without telling his wife where he was going, and she was concerned about that, but gone he was, and Spencer would have to wait. Spencer had no patience for waiting. He was used to fast food and fast service from his employees. Butler was fast becoming an employee, instead of a trusted confidant, Spencer thought with disappointment, and he had a renewed feeling of isolation reminiscent of his time investigating Billy McBride.

When Spencer arrived at his office, his first concern was whether Butler had called, and Amy reported that he had not, but he did call his wife. Spencer was somewhat relieved to hear from Amy that Butler's wife did call and told her that Butler was taking the rest of Friday off and was out until Monday, instead of out indefinitely. Nothing more was said. With high anxiety over the possible loss of a friend and employee at a time he could least afford it, Spencer looked for any distraction to get his mind off the Simpson case and his belief that he had solved a major part of the case with no way to act on it. Unless he could convince Butler of the soundness of his logic from what he had, it would be just another useless theory with no one along for the ride, if he acted alone.

Spencer was convinced he was right about Rollins but doing nothing might be his only option. Doing anything with other authorities would surely mean a dead end for the Simpson baby. For the first time, he realized that without Butler along, there was no confirmation for doing something within all the possibilities the two might consider, legal and perhaps not so legal, to save the Simpson child. Without Butler, there was no one left, except Spencer's father, whom he could always call for bedrock logic he always felt he could live with, or die with, if necessary. Now was the time for that call.

"Hello, Dad. Got a minute?"

"You know I do, Son. What's on your mind?"

"I've got another situation. I can't go into all the details, but I know I might be the only person that knows someone involved with the Simpson baby kidnapping. I can do nothing or do something on my own. Either way, a lot of bad things might happen. It's hard to weigh out, and I guess I just need some of your country wisdom."

145

"Did I ever train you to get my permission to do the right thing? Is that what you are really asking for?"

"Well, the training wheels are off, Dad. It does feel like I'm asking permission, but I think I'm just letting you know that whatever comes of this, I will have thought through the consequences."

"The real measure of a man is not what he acquires or the comfort of his life. The measure is how well he can live with himself with the decisions he makes. If the life of someone is a part of that decision, then you alone will have to live with the consequences. You once told me that you never would do anything that you could not at least explain to a federal judge. Well, whatever you do, just be prepared to explain honestly whatever it is that you do legally, or illegally, if that's what this is leading up to. I thought you understood that in the McBride case. I have lived my whole life believing in what I learned as a child from my dad, and I thought I passed that on to you – that bad things happen when good men do nothing. I thought I taught you that much."

"I did learn that. It's just that there's a big difference sometimes between learning and doing."

"The measure of the man is the 'doing' part, and I've always thought you measured up. You'll never prove me wrong, Son. You talk about being alone in all this. I thought your investigator has always been a big help. Where's he on this?"

"I'm working on it. He's not too impressed with me right now. When he sees me going it alone, he might change his mind. The important thing is that I don't want you disappointed in me, if what I have to do costs me my job and perhaps a lot more. I don't even know what I can do, but I know I will do something with or without my investigator and perhaps with or without the law."

"Son, I'd be lying if I said I'm not worried, but nothing makes me prouder than I am right now, knowing I brought you up to know what is important in life. Whatever road you take, you will have to live with it. That's a heavy burden and why I always warn against grinding into the quick. I'd hate to see you getting kicked in the head. Then again, there might be no other place to go and try to prepare for it. Nothing you do will ever disappoint me."

"I'll keep you posted. One way or another, I know you will be hearing more about this, and I'll do my best to get to you first. Fair enough?"

"Fair enough. I'll wait for the call."

MONDAY

8:15 A.M.

Chapter Seventeen

Monday could not arrive soon enough for Spencer. He felt the urgency of his solution in spite of Butler's objection. It was the tenth day after the assault with little of substance accomplished. He had spent the weekend polishing his argument to deliver to Butler on his return, if he returned as expected. Butler made several calls to Spencer's cell phone during the weekend and Spencer ignored them. Whatever was to be said between them, Spencer decided, would have to be said man to man and in person. As he sat in his office, he considered his approach would have to be different and would begin with an apology for implying that Butler was in the pocket of Rollins. Spencer never believed it, but implying it was the most destructive and thoughtless statement he could make to his most trusted investigator and one he considered one of those few friends anyone really has. If unsuccessful, he would have to plan on going it alone.

"Butler's here. Should I send him in?" Amy asked.

That question alone spelled trouble, Spencer thought. Ordinarily, Butler would not wait for Amy to announce his presence.

"Yes, please," Spencer answered.

"Morning, Boss. I tried to call you and you weren't answering. I've got something you need to hear," Butler said as he casually walked into Spencer's office for what Spencer thought was a showdown or another dress down.

"Me first," Spencer said looking down and announcing his confession to follow. "I was wrong about you covering for Rollins. It sounded worse than I meant it to be. I was just thinking about that cop to cop loyalty thing, and it came out wrong. I still think I'm right about his involvement, but I took your disagreement out on you, and I apologize for that. I hope we can get back on track. Whatever you have to say, I hope it's

149

not about quitting."

Butler looked puzzled and took what seemed like minutes before answering. Finally, he said, "We need to kill Rollins."

Shocked, Spencer asked, "You're not serious?"

"No, I'm not serious, but we should kill him, if there is any justice in this."

"I think you've been out in the sun too long. From the looks of things, you did get some sun," Spencer said laughing. "Where did you go for your short vacation?"

"Key West, Florida. I have to admit, I was upset with you, and just like you started out with McBride, I was intent on proving you wrong. To be totally honest about it, I planned on shoving your crazy solution up your farrier son's ass. I thought the best place to start was with your Rollins' boat idea. Other than words, that's all you had. I figured I'd show you there was nothing to it but an old empty tub. I traced his boat through Florida registration to a marina in Key West. It's a city marina with a lot of boats, but I found it and guess who was on board?"

"Rollins?"

"No. Four guys that look like they're from the Middle East, just as you suspected, but here's the clincher. One of the guys had a vertical scar from his forehead down to his eye and had the blackest eyes I've ever seen. So far, everything fit from the boat registration description, but I still couldn't be sure without seeing the registration number on the boat or its name on the transom. There wasn't a woman on board that I could see either."

"You had to look like a cop. Did you approach them? How close did you get?"

"I was just walking down the boat ramp and looking at the boats. It was hard to see the registration numbers, and I just walked up to these guys sitting at the back of the boat that fit the description on the registration. There weren't a lot of people around. Seems that on a good day everyone with a boat is out fishing. I just walked by, and then I had an idea. I turned and said, 'You guys interested in renting your boat for fishing today?' At first, I don't think they understood me, so I repeated the question. The one with the scar and black eyes then said, 'No,' and I pressed him with some bullshit about how hard it is to find a boat to rent. While I did that, I looked over the boat and saw the registration number on the left side. You farm boys wouldn't know it, but that's called the port side in nautical talk, and it was a match. I also saw the boat name on the transom, and it said Tortuga, but that didn't match with turtle you told me.

"Tortuga is Spanish for turtle. I should have told you. Sorry."

"It worked out and it gets better. When I walked off the pier, there was a Cuban seafood market nearby with a neat slogan that caught my eye. It said, "We buy your catch or sell what you say you caught!" I guess we fishermen are not very honest when it comes to size and quantity. Anyway, I went in and asked if they had any Tortuga just to find out casually what it meant and he said, 'It's illegal to sell sea turtles and they haven't sold them for many years.' That really cinched it. Sorry for the 'farm kid' remark Friday. I was dying to get a photo, but these guys were watching me closely, and I had to appear uninterested in them. All things considered, I got enough to owe you an apology. I hope you will accept it. I'm a lot older than you and apologizing to someone half my age isn't easy. I hate the taste of crow and never had a good recipe for it."

"Are you kidding?" Spencer answered. "Put all that in the rearview mirror. Do you think the woman, or the baby was there? Perhaps inside?"

"I doubt it. I watched from a distance and never saw her or the baby. It's not a very big boat, maybe twenty-eight feet at best with some sort of small cabin, and probably no air conditioner from what I saw. There was no electric service going from the boat to the dock to run it. It reminded me of that old boat in the movie 'Key Largo' with Humphrey Bogart. Those old boats are hotter than blazes inside during the day in Key West without AC. If she and the baby were there, they would have been outside with the others for sure. To make it look good, I walked on every boat ramp within eyesight of those guys and asked the few people there about renting. I don't know what I would have done, if someone agreed, but that never happened. I think it's a safe bet the woman and the baby are somewhere else. Finding her is going to be tough."

"I think keeping an eye on those guys will be job one. It would be a hell of a note, if the woman and the baby showed up just after you left," Spencer concluded after thinking through his options. "Whatever we do, I need you here, and I have to bring someone in now to observe the boat. The baby could show up at any time, and there will have to be fast action. Who to get for that and how much to tell, are my questions now. Any suggestions?" Spencer asked.

"You want to bring in another investigator?"

"No. They're all great, but too great. This whole thing will get overthought, if I do that. I just need someone that will do exactly what they are told and nothing more. Is the boat hard to find without you being along?"

"No. Here's the good part. I was able to get a phone picture of the pier and the boat in the distance. A picture is worth a thousand boats. You can see those guys without much detail, but the picture makes finding it easy. I'll have an 8x10 made up before noon."

"There's an assistant that told me last week that he has my back. I think I'll send him on a little vacation. I want you here when I talk it over with him, okay?"

"You're the Boss. I'll never forget that again, and that's a promise. I guess we now need to figure out what to do with Rollins," Butler said. "He's a player, but how much? Considering all of our options on what to do with him, you don't want to know what I'm thinking."

"Let's not go there," Spencer said, "but I think I'm reading your mind. I need to think this through on how to open him up. I wish it were as simple as just taking all this to his boss, but then there is possible involvement there, too. I'm sure Mc-Givney would love to get his hands on this, but I think we would end up with a dead baby or no baby. It's going to end up on us, if we're not careful, like when the press tried to pin Thomas and the nurse on us. It's been ten days now from the assault, and time is running out. Did you get anywhere with that hospital ICU check? That would solve everything, if we had the baby."

"Nothing but dry holes, but I'm working on it. I checked Key West. Nothing makes sense, because if the baby was in a hospital there, I would've seen the woman on the boat with the others. I'll go back and work through the hospitals here. You're a pretty creative guy. How about you come up with a plan for Rollins. Let me know when you want to talk with someone you want to send down to Key West."

"It's Arnold. I'll get him now and do my best to keep it simple. All he needs to know is where to go, what to look for and what to report to me. He won't be happy about being in the dark, but he'll have to get used to it."

"You called it with Rollins. Don't expect me to disagree on this one. I'm sure you've thought it through and I'm okay with him in this, if you are."

"Amy," Spencer called out. "I need Arnold and tell him it's urgent."

Within minutes, Arnold appeared at Spencer's door.

"Come in, Arnold. I have a job for you. It's all legal, not that it would be anything else, and I need you to start now. You're going to Key West. Take the first available flight. Buy clothes when you get there. An island shirt and shorts will work and tell no one where you're going and what you're doing. Bring a hat. Are you with me so far?"

"I am. Can I ask a question?"

"Actually, no. When you get there, you are going to keep an eye on a boat and its occupants. I think that there are four men on board. Soon, possibly, there will be a woman arriving and possibly a baby. Your job is to look for those last two and call me immediately if either one shows up – a baby or a woman. If the boat moves with a baby on board, I want you to call the Monroe County sheriff in Key West and report a kidnapping. Tell the sheriff you work for me, and I'll take his call, if necessary, but try not to waste time with introductions. Give the sheriff the details you see about the boat and its direction when leaving. You have to make sure he understands that the baby onboard has been kidnapped. That's your most important job, and I need you to do it without question. Amy will set you up with a credit card, and she'll make the call for a flight. Can you do this?"

"Count me in, Boss. Can I ask how I'm supposed to find the boat?"

"That's why Butler's here, and he has all the details right down to a photograph of the location. Play the part of a tourist. It worked for Butler. Just find a spot to read a newspaper and enjoy the sun. I hear it's hot down there. I want you to go with Butler now to his office to give you the lay of the land, literally, and give you a photo that will help get you orientated to find the boat. Call Butler with your flight details and call him again when you find the boat. For the time being, there's no return date. I know it's asking a lot, but I need you to do this, and I trust you."

Arnold left with Butler after receiving the office credit card. Even though he was in the dark on the most important reasons for his trip to Key West, Arnold took great pride in finally being on the inside of a top-secret investigation. He may have had reasonable suspicions that it was all related to the Simpson kidnapping, but he never asked and never let on. It was the one question he was not permitted to ask.

Spencer considered that he had come a long way in two days of total uncertainty. Lunch was still a couple of hours off, but a trip over to Alibis wouldn't hurt to tell Kayleigh how well his apology went, even if Butler made it unnecessary. She didn't need to know the details of that, but he needed to tell her how valuable her opinion was and that he followed through with her advice.

As Spencer entered the bar, a voice called out that he recognized. It was Officer Jim Fields.

"Hey, Spencer. Come on over. I have someone I want you to meet."

"Give me a minute. I need to talk with Kayleigh, and who do you think comes first?"

There was a chorus of several officers who answered in unison, "Kayleigh."

"Hi, Kayleigh. I just wanted to stop by and thank you for the good advice concerning Butler. Yes, I did apologize, and it all worked out."

"Glad to help out. Now that you fixed that, you must have some free time, right?"

It was a question he hoped for, and his answer is one he dreaded. Surely, Kayleigh was asking if he now had time for her and this one visit might just be his last before she went back to school.

"No. No time. Something has come up, and as much as I want to chase you down, just to let you know how I feel about you; I might not be back before you go back to school."

Kayleigh began to tear up and said, "You don't have to chase me down, you caught me the first time we met. If it works that way for us, I'm going to miss you. Maybe it's for the best. I need to keep my mind on my studies before taking on law school."

"How far away are you going for that?" Spencer asked.

"I'm going to Georgetown Law in Washington, D.C., and I plan on giving you a run for your money when I get admitted."

"If you don't get me admitted first," Spencer said, letting her know the depth of his feeling for her. "I better go over and check out Jim Fields before I say too much that will get me in trouble with Finnegan."

"Do you realize we haven't even had a date?" Kayleigh said.

"You're forgetting the first time we met, and you picked me up on the street."

"If that counts, it's your turn."

"Well done, my almost attorney friend," Spencer said smugly. "It's my turn and count on going out with me before you go back. There, I finally said it, and I'm looking forward to it. Do me a favor, though, and let your dad know that I will be 'a-callin'."

"Okay, coward," she said smiling. For both of them, flirting was over, but there was little time now for anything else. Spencer looked at Kayleigh, closed his eyes to remember her and turned toward Jim Fields to meet someone who wanted to meet him.

"Mister Prosecutor, I want you to meet the G.I. Joe I told you about."

"You're Joe Walcott, the guy who found the Simpson woman," Spencer said.

"That I am. Glad to meet you. I read about you, and I want you to know how much I respect what you do."

"It's really the other way around. I heard about your service in Vietnam, and I want to thank you for it."

"It wasn't always that way, you know. I'm one of those guys that got spit on when I landed stateside. No parades for us. We just got a lot of bad memories over there and more when we got home. The people there got a new and improved country, and I got PTSD. I'm not complaining, but I always come back to the question of what we got out of all the men and women that got killed or screwed up over there?"

"I don't have an answer on that one, but I know you were tested in the fire and came out a winner, as far as I'm concerned, because you lived through it, even if our country cut and ran. It's hard to get the memory of the last helicopter out of Saigon out of my head with all those people trying to escape, even though I wasn't born when that photo was taken."

"Every one of us who served got tested, and maybe that test was more than most know. We were tested on our ability to survive, and that meant killing the enemy any way we could. I think we all went a little crazy doing that. You might think it was criminal."

"What do you mean?"

"Did you serve?" Walcott asked hesitatingly before going further with any details of his service.

"No. We were between wars when I was in college, and it was a volunteer army by then. I have to tell you that I have always felt some guilt by not serving."

That answer was enough for Joe and he felt confident he was among friends.

"I was an Army Ranger," Joe began, "and my skill was as a paratrooper, but when we first teamed up with the Marines at Chu Lai, we had to defend a southern border of our installation. It wasn't like the movies where the enemy attacked during the day and we just fought back. We had night vision.

It was in its infancy, but it worked. So, we're defending on a wall at night, and with our green night vision, we could see the enemy crawling up the hill to kill us. I had plenty of time to think about what I was going to do next. I wasn't trained for what happened next. It was just reaction in slow motion. It was shooting fish in a barrel. We picked our shots. We talked it over, 'I get the two on the right and the two behind them.' A buddy would take the others, and they all died in twenty seconds. Then we would do it all over again. Fortunately, blood flows downhill."

"I'm surprised you talk about that stuff. I always hear about the World War II vets who never talked about how bad it was fighting the Nazis."

"There's some of that, but not with me. Those guys knew they were saving the country from the Nazis and had to do it. They had what you call the 'moral authority'. We never felt we were saving anything except our own asses and the ass of our buddies. There wasn't much moral authority over there, unless you were a general calling shots from the rear or watching through heavy lenses. Sure, I talk about it. If I don't talk about it, I got nothing. I still need to talk about it. Do you understand that?"

"I think so," Spencer said, recalling how Molly McBride cursed him every chance she had for the wrongful prosecution of her son before his scheduled execution even though Spencer had nothing to do with it. That too, was all she had, he thought. "Do you have any regrets for the people you killed?"

"Never. What they did to us, when we were caught, was beyond war crimes. It was savagery, pure and simple, and designed to scare the shit out of us. It worked, but we got even. That doesn't happen in these more modern times. Now you get prosecuted for getting even. No offense. We did what we had to do to survive. I remember going along in a Hughey helicopter with two high-value Vietcong. They knew what we needed, and they wouldn't talk. They laughed at us. Stupid Americans, right? We had morals, right? Or so they thought. We had a creed, but morals weren't a part of it. My captain said, 'Give that one some airtime.'"

"What did that mean, 'airtime'?" Spencer asked.

"We were about 2,500 feet above the ground, and I threw out the one he pointed at. He got airtime for about a half mile down, and the other one sang like Linda Ronstadt. He never stopped talking and telling everything, even after we got back on the ground. It saved our lives to learn what he told us, and we weren't going to get it any other way. So much for moral values, and when it's real war, not some textbook war, there are times when the means justify the ends. The fact is, we all knew it was a crime. I knew I murdered that guy. He wasn't the last one either, and we did it anyway to save ourselves. Survival trumps crimes. The creed of a Ranger is to lead the way, and sometimes those little son-of-a-bitches had to lead the way down for us to survive. Just don't get caught. That's the real war time lesson, and don't you forget it. Don't ever try to make war and survival more than the horror show that it is. When someone tries to kill you, kill back. Real simple. The 'airtime' deal made the rounds with the enemy, and it wasn't long before we would push two into the Hughey and they would both start singing before we left the ground."

"Did you ever push out one of those who talked anyway?"

Joe paused for a moment looking at Spencer stone faced and said, "Hell no! It was always about the objective. Murder wasn't the objective. Information was the objective. In the field, killing was the objective, and I never had much time to consider if it was murder to kill the guy trying his best to kill me, but there were plenty of times when all that got blurred between right and wrong. Before long, we just didn't think about right and wrong, unless we had a new second lieutenant leading on point who was probably about to get shot after giving us his lecture on field ethics."

As Spencer listened, the seeds of a plan were taking hold, and he pressed further.

"Do you think you could do all that again under the right circumstances?" It was a verb without a noun but made for a little humor from those listening.

"Okay, Spencer, who do you want to throw out of a helicopter?" Fields asked humorously without a hint of his question's significance to Spencer.

"That's a tough one. So many reporters, and so little time," Spencer successfully added to the laugh and distraction.

"Here's how it is. I'm the same guy now that I was when I got back. Fortunately, I don't have a beef with reporters," Walcott said, finishing on a high note.

"I believe it," Spencer said. "I read the report that you went over the fence to that ambulance with a Winchester."

"And you probably read that I would have used it, if I had a chance. No doubt there. There's no crime in thinking about what I would like to do to those guys. For better or worse, it's who I am. It's what my country made me, and I'm damn proud of it even if my country now hates me for it."

Spencer did not have a specific plan, but the tools were laid out for him by Joe, who was a trained, but aging killer. Spencer did not know how he could be used but felt there had to be a way to use him without committing murder or conspiring to commit murder. He needed time to put the pieces together.

"Are you still jumping out of airplanes?"

"Once a month, weather permitting. I can't explain it. It's not a thrill ride. It's freedom, man, at terminal velocity. I never feel freer than I do in free fall from 10,000 feet. I know it sounds crazy, and guys like me won't admit it, but we hate to pull the cord. We hate to see the jump end."

"What's terminal velocity?" Spencer asked. "Sounds deadly."

"It is, if you hit the ground at that speed. Terminal velocity is the maximum speed a free-falling object like me can reach given the height of the drop, air resistance, temperature and other atmospheric conditions. Basically, the speed of a falling object stops accelerating faster and faster because of air resistance, and a maximum speed is reached if there is enough distance left between the object and the ground. It's something jumpers consider. At 10,000 feet or more, a guy my size with head down and diving toward the earth he'll usually reach about 150 to 180 miles per hour as a maximum velocity and hit the ground at that speed, if he don't pull the rip cord. At 150 miles per hour, that's quite a ride for a while. Now, if

159

he flattens out, he may only reach 120 miles per hour and the result will be the same without the rip cord," he said smiling.

"Does a person's weight make a difference?"

"No. Basic law of physics. All objects fall at the same rate regardless of weight in a vacuum. It's air resistance that makes a difference. The rest is the law of gravity and the one I survive by."

"Ever worry about the chute not opening?" Spencer queried.

"Sure, but that's why I pack the chute myself and the reserve."

"What's a reserve?"

"It's a reserve chute called an AAD. That stands for Automatic Activation Device. It's tucked away like a fanny pack, and you never see it, unlike the main chute that fits on your back. That's the one you see in the movies. When it fails, the reserve kicks in and pops out at a preset altitude with the modern equipment now available. 'Look Mom, no hands!' The reserve does it all on its own, if the main doesn't open. It's a great system and has saved many lives, especially for beginners. The reserve chute is not as large as the main, and it can be a hard landing, but you will walk away from it instead of being picked up in pieces."

"That's a sobering thought. The pieces, I mean. I also know your days are spent farming, but would you mind if I dropped by to talk to you about what you saw when you helped Mrs. Simpson?"

"I don't mind, but I think I gave the sheriff everything I could remember."

"I understand, but I would like to hear it for myself. It's quite a story, and you saved Mrs. Simpson, from what the doctors said. You've got to be proud of that."

"I suppose, but I wish I could have done something to save that baby, too."

"I'll look forward to talking with you. Who knows? Maybe there is something that will come out of it. Do you mind if I stop by tomorrow?"

"Just tell me when, but two o'clock works best for me."

"I'll be at your farmhouse at two and thanks again," Spencer promised, as Walcott turned and walked toward the door.

"What did I tell you about G.I. Joe? One of a kind. I knew you'd like to meet him," Fields volunteered.

"You have no idea," Spencer answered without more, but for him the threads of a plan were pulling together "like the cords on a parachute," he mused to himself. By morning, he hoped, he would have a first run of a plan that he could live with.

TUESDAY

8:00 A.M.

Chapter Eighteen

Butler was waiting at Spencer's office the next morning, day eleven after the assault. Butler had also given thought to a plan, and he was anxious to share it. He also got calls from Arnold, and nothing had changed at the boat from what Butler observed in Key West.

"Boss, I think I've got the best solution, and by the way, Arnold is faithfully manning his post of duty. He's really getting into his role, and I think he's gone native. He hasn't shaved since he got to Key West, bought an island shirt, a straw hat, shorts and hooked up one of those fake gold earrings. This is where it gets good. He bought a watercolor paint kit, including an easel and stool, and hangs out at the boat pier pretending to be an artist while watching the boat. He told me that so far he's sold two paintings to Chinese tourists and was hit on by three guys. He wants out of there, but he's calling around for a motel with a view of the dock. I told him to go ahead and buy field glasses if he finds a place."

"Can he actually paint?" Spencer asked.

"Not a stroke. He said he's just putting a lot of paint on paper, and the tourists think he's a Picasso!"

"At least we don't have to worry about Arnold. What's your best solution?" Spencer asked. "I have a plan, too, but you first. Might be a good idea to shut my door, though. I don't think Amy needs to hear what we're talking about."

Butler shut the door and began his recitation of his plan.

"First, we have to accept that Rollins is guilty of conspiracy to commit two murders, one attempted murder and a kidnapping, even if he wasn't there when it all went down. Second, he knows where the baby is, and his boat is going to be the instrument for delivery. These two concepts are important because whatever we do to get the truth out of him, he can't ever be in a position to rat us out without taking himself down. We really don't need to murder him. I don't think either one of us is into that, but we will need to assault him, and that's a serious federal crime, as you know. Again, I think we're insulated. We get what we need, find the baby and turn Rollins loose."

"You make it sound so easy, but what happens when he just says, 'Fuck you'? He tells the guys on the boat to split, and the woman and baby never show up. We then have that big pile of shit you were convinced I was working on and a federal indictment for felony assault on a federal officer, torture and who knows what else. I never thought I would ever say, 'I'm okay with committing a felony,' especially to you, a former police officer and my chief investigator. I know we're getting deep into this, but my conscience is not telling me to stop. I keep asking myself though, 'Why should I care? Why should I get involved?' But I can't shake it off that I do care, and I will get involved. Is there something wrong with me?" Spencer asked more rhetorically than hoping for reassurance.

"I don't think so, but I'm not your moral compass. Remember, the first thing I told you was we need to kill Rollins," Butler said laughing and joined in by Spencer to shake off the reality of the plan that was taking hold.

"Whatever we do to Rollins," Spencer said, picking up on the thread, "short of killing him or leaving marks, he has to be convinced he will die a horrible death, and there's a crime in that. We can't leave any evidence, and it has to be his word against ours. Just the same, I think I have just the thing. In fact, it's so outrageous that no one would ever believe Rollins, even if he tries to prosecute us. Everything you said about the first two concepts is true. He is a criminal and he does know where the baby is. That's why we can risk the consequences of the crimes we will probably commit, if we put a plan into action. If I get caught and can't lie my way out of this, I have thought about the reality of facing a federal judge and answering his last question before he sends me to prison, 'What the hell were you thinking?' I know I'll get the lecture. I already understand that I'm throwing my life away and will rot in a federal prison as an example of why people like me, with the position I hold, cannot forsake the law. I know the consequences; in case you're wondering if I've thought this through. I can't seem to say 'no'. Maybe it's just not real yet. Maybe it's just theoretical and hasn't sunk in, but I have to do this somehow. We need to make this work and not get caught. If it does, I'll worry about my failed ethics, morality and criminality after we get that baby back to the Simpsons."

"For what it's worth, I thought it through, too," Butler chimed in. "Not so eloquently, but thoroughly. The weakest part of any plan is always secrecy. You know that from every prosecution you've ever been involved in. Arnold might be a weak link, but I don't think he knows jack shit about what we're up to. When I gave him the directions, I expected him to ask if it was about the Simpson case. I think he knows, but he never asked. I think he will stay dumb and on board. My concern is who else we might have to involve with real details? Whatever the plan, it's going to take more than the two of us to trap and catch Rollins, if that's what it takes. What's your plan?" Butler asked.

"It all came together last night after I went to Alibis, and it's going to take two more for a total of four, excluding Arnold. He will always be on the outside, and I want to keep it that way. The first new guy is Joe Walcott. Remember him from the Simpson case? He's a Vietnam veteran and a former Army Ranger with a specialty in parachuting. I met him for the first-time last night, and he wishes he could have done more to save the Simpson's baby. This will be his chance. I think he has his own code, or creed, and it's different than our criminal code. My plan was hatched when he was reminiscing about his exploits with the VC. He told of throwing one out of a helicopter in front of a second prisoner who refused to talk. He called it giving the one he threw out 'airtime,' and the other couldn't stop talking after that. Now here's the outrageous part. We're going to give Rollins a plane ride, and that's where our fourth guy comes in as a pilot – nothing more. Just the same, the pilot has to be in on everything to pull this off."

"So, who gets thrown out of the plane?"

"Don't worry, it won't be you. It's not me either, and it sure as hell won't be the pilot. It's Walcott wearing a hood, gagged, wearing a winter coat, handcuffed and with a cement block tied to his ankles. Rollins will be bound also, and in the same way, but without the hood, so he can see everything we will do to Walcott without any idea of who he is. As we climb to an altitude over a river, Rollins is going to learn that we know it's him, and we'll tell him the mystery man wearing the hood is also involved but won't talk. I'll ask Rollins to talk. He'll say 'no'. He'll say we're not going to kill anyone, and then I'll push Walcott out. That should loosen Rollins up. What he will not know is that Walcott will be wearing a reserve chute under his coat, and it will deploy at a preset altitude. Walcott explained all that to me when I showed a lot of interest in parachuting. That's when things started to gel. Before the chute opens, he will be able to free his hands, pull off his hood and cut away the cement block. Then he steers for a landing and calls in. If Rollins doesn't crack, we'll just take him back, drop him off and wish him a good day. I'm convinced he won't say a word against us."

"No 'Plan B'?" Butler asked.

"Not really, but what do you think of my plan so far, assuming we don't need a 'Plan B'?"

"Like you said, I think it's so outrageous, it's great. I hope he falls for it!"

"Nice pun, but appropriate. What I forgot to tell you is that Rollins said he likes boating because he's afraid of heights, and altitude might be enough to bring him around."

"I have to admit, it scares me just thinking about it. But if it fails and he clams up, what happens to the baby and the guys in Florida. Seems like a big risk on that end."

"It is, but it's all we've got. What we have will never get any better than this. There won't be a 'Plan B' unless I kill Rollins and that's not happening. The plan's a risk we have to take. I'll make it convincing enough."

"We'll have to find a pilot and a plane to rent, and I don't know where to start on that one," Butler said.

"I do. I think I have just the guy to give me a lead on a pilot and maybe a lead on a plane. I'll start work on that next,"
166

Spencer said. "What I would like you to do is figure out how we can lure Rollins away from his office alone and how we can overtake him without getting shot. It's a new world out there, and its amazing how many cameras are out there watching. It seems that every shopkeeper has some sort of camera recording both inside and out. Many houses now have one of those doorbell cameras for the porch pirates, and the last thing we need is to see ourselves on the Six O'clock News attacking and kidnapping an FBI agent.

"You get the plane and pilot. I'll figure out the rest," Butler assured him.

***

Following his planning session with Butler, Spencer knew that his first and best option for finding a pilot was Chuck Smith, the bailiff of Judge Macintosh. Spencer and Smith killed a lot of time waiting out jury verdicts talking about Smith's flying background, so Smith might be able to provide a lead on a pilot with a compromised set of moral and ethical values. How to approach Smith on that now seemed more challenging than the plan itself. "How do I ask Smith if he knows anyone willing to help assault and kidnap an FBI agent?" Spencer thought to himself with a sense of how foolhardy the reality was. "And by the way, I need an airplane to pull this off. Any ideas where I can find one?" as he continued his self-examination and critique. The thought of such questions finally struck home regarding how absurd and illegal his conspiracy with Butler had taken shape. There was no easy way to ask anyone the questions he had, he concluded. By the time he arrived at Judge Macintosh's courtroom, Spencer knew he could not approach Smith for help, and he was about to turn back when Smith called out to him.

"Good to see you, Spencer. Any chance we'll get a crack at the Simpson kidnapping case? Anything you can tell me?"

"I wish there were. There's a few good leads, but the one who knows won't talk, and legally there's no way to make that happen."

"How about a little truth serum?"

"I wish I could, but I'd be the one going to prison instead of the bad guy."

"So, who has to know?" Smith responded, and Spencer began to see an opening for further review of Smith's outlook.

"I would know, and that should be enough, but I have to tell you I am tempted to break some laws to find out. Keep that to yourself, but what do you think of me for that position?" Spencer asked.

"Seems you broke a few rules when you caught Herald and saved that McBride fellow from certain death. I won't mention it, but I think you were right, and I have always been proud to know you after that. I don't think that made you a criminal, even if it was a crime. Sometimes, you just have to stand up and be counted. We did a lot of that standing up in the Marines, and I'm proud of that, too."

Spencer had heard enough to risk going into what he was planning and needed to extract a promise from a Marine with his Marine values never to divulge what Spencer was about to say, if Smith could not help.

"Colonel Smith, what I am about to tell you has to stay here and never see the light of day, even if what I am about to tell you involves what made you proud of me before. Will you promise me that?"

"I swear. Now what the hell is it? What have you gotten yourself into this time?"

"I'm here because I need your help finding a contact for a crime I'm going to commit. If that's a game changer, I'll stop now, and this meeting never happened, okay?"

"Nothing's changed, Go on."

"I know who participated as a co-conspirator in the murder of Dr. Thomas, his nurse and the attempted murder of Mrs. Simpson. He's also a co-conspirator in the kidnapping of the Simpson baby, but I can't risk trying to prove it in court or to his superiors. They may be involved, too. Right now, four of his co-conspirators are on his boat waiting for a fifth conspirator to bring the baby and leave the country. The co-conspirator here could be forced to talk, but if I don't force him now, we may lose the baby. I'm not planning truth serum. That's movie stuff. It's too dangerous, and I'm not in this to murder anyone,
168

but I will force him to talk."

"What do you need me for?"

"I'm getting to that. This guy is afraid of heights, and I am planning to enlist the aid of an old Army Ranger who still is into parachuting. I'm going to take the guy for a ride in an airplane and throw out the Ranger disguised as another co-conspirator, hood and all, along with a cement block tied to his leg. The Ranger will have a well-disguised reserve chute, but the bad guy will think he's next, if he doesn't start talking. From what I know, it should work, and if not, there is no way the bad guy will complain without ratting himself out.

"Where did you get this idea, Spencer? I know it's not original. It has Vietnam written all over it. I was there, too. I heard about it. I never did it, but I have to tell you, I had no problem with it. Some did. I didn't."

"The guy I plan to enlist with the parachute gave a VC what he called 'airtime'."

"That's the expression I heard about, too. I think he's telling it straight; you never hear about it. It was murder, but it did work. We didn't deal too much with right and wrong over there. Bad place to be. It screwed up your head, and I always hated to read about the soldiers prosecuted who were caught. The lucky ones weren't, and there were plenty of them."

"What I need from you is a contact for a pilot that would be willing to participate in this and a way to get a plane. I know it's asking a lot, and I can't imagine how you would even approach someone on this. I was just about to walk away myself, thinking how crazy this is, when you called me over."

"It is crazy, and I haven't been so excited about anything since combat," Smith admitted. "I think I'm thanking you for this. I want in, and the irony is that we could use the judge's plane. It's perfect. It seats six, and four sit in the back in what is called club seating. Two face forward and two face backward with a small table in between. There's a door there that splits vertically in half. I'll remove the rear half of it so it will be windy and noisy. I'll have to remove that half of the door because we could never open it in the slip stream. I'll also remove the table. It will be perfect to get the guy into the plane and push out the other guy with the parachute. It's called a Beechcraft A36, if you want to look it up. It's a great plane, and I have to exercise it every two weeks to keep it oiled and the electrons circulating in the radios, regardless of whether the judge needs it or not. He'll never know if it's gone for a little 'airtime'."

"Here's a little more irony for you to consider. The person that I'm trying to scare the hell out of is an FBI agent heading for an illegally paid retirement. Does that change anything?"

"Do I know him?" Smith asked.

"I doubt it. His name is John Rollins."

"Don't know him, and I wouldn't give a damn, even if I did. When do we get this off the ground, so to speak?"

"That's the second good pun I've heard today about flying, and again, it fits. I have to get with the Ranger and get him on board. I'm thinking two days, but our time window is shortening. We expect that there is some health problem with the baby that has held up the transfer, and that could end at any moment. I'll get back with you just as soon as I pull it all together."

"I'll start working on my part tonight. By the way, do you think you can get this done with just you, me, and the Ranger? Do you have anyone else that's in on this?"

As Spencer was walking away to get with the Ranger, he turned, smiled and said, "Butler, of course!"

Chapter Nineteen

Spencer considered that the worst had to be over by obtaining Smith's involvement. He had to know what he was getting into and never blinked or expressed a second thought about consequences or his conscience. It should have been harder to convince Smith to join in, he thought, and Spencer never considered Smith as a likely candidate for his new adventure. Nevertheless, he was all in, and he hoped Joe Walcott would see it the same way. After all, Spencer concluded, they weren't going to kill Rollins, even if street justice might demand it, and in the final analysis, Rollins should appreciate he had earned what was coming. For Spencer, a felony or two on his lawyerly conscious would be a small price to pay. As for the others, with the return of the Simpson baby, they may have to pay no price at all.

Walcott would be the last to be involved, if he also agreed, so Spencer took the rest of the day to find Walcott at his farm. It was nearing two in the afternoon for his scheduled meeting with him, and the drive was relaxing. Spencer already had a handle on Walcott's frame of mind concerning the Simpson case, and it was just a matter of seeing if Walcott was the real deal or "all hat and no cattle," as Spencer's dad said of what he called "bullshit artists".

When Spencer arrived, Walcott was working on a tractor parked in front of his farmhouse.

"Hello, Mr. Prosecutor," Walcott said, as he took a towel and cleaned grease off his hands. "You might not want to shake this old farmer's hand right now. This type of grease doesn't come off easy, and it smells. What's on your mind?" Walcott asked, careful not to extend his hand.

"I'm a farm kid, too, and it's good clean grease as far as I'm concerned. Always proud to shake the hand of a working man," Spencer said ingratiatingly, as he extended his hand in friendship. It was eagerly accepted by Walcott with a powerful grip.

"I'm going to take a chance and tell you something in the strictest confidence. I can't force you to keep what I'm about to say secret, but it will hurt some good people, if you don't. The best I will be able to do is deny that I ever spoke to you about what I'm about to say. Does that work for you? Can we have that understanding?"

"Stop now if you want me to kill someone. There was a joke yesterday about reporters. If that's your problem, forget it. I'm not into that shit," Walcott said sternly and with conviction.

"No one is going to get killed, unless it's you."

"Okay. You have my attention. What's this all about?"

"I know who the Simpson kidnappers are, basically, and where they are, at least most of them. Right now, I think four are waiting for one of them to show up with the Simpson baby on a boat in Key West. My plan is to find out where the baby is now, and that's where you come in. Still interested?"

"Yeah, but what do you mean that you know basically who they are?"

"There are four Middle East looking guys on a boat, and one matches the description given by Mrs. Simpson before she was put into an induced coma. It's not just a good match. It's a perfect match. And what are those four guys doing just hanging out on a boat in Key West owned by the FBI agent who's on the Simpson case?" Spencer asked to elicit the obvious understanding of Rollins' involvement.

"I read Mrs. Simpson came to and never saw or remembered anything."

"That was a lie, and I can't tell you more. My source swore me to secrecy. I know you wouldn't want me to violate that."

"So, what do you need from me, if you're not hiring my Winchester and military background?"

"Your background, yes. Winchester, no. I need your parachuting skills essentially to scare someone into telling me where the baby is. There's a reason the baby hasn't arrived at the boat. As a premature birth, a month early, I think there's
172

a hold up because of a medical problem. The delay is coming to an end soon, if I'm right."

"You had my attention, but now you have my interest. Do I jump with someone? That can be dangerous and scary without training."

"No. You jump alone. The scary part is that the person I'm after is an FBI agent who's in on the murders and kidnapping. Is that a deal breaker?"

"Not yet, but it's a lot to process. What are you, a prosecutor, doing? It's criminal stuff you're talking about."

"More than anyone else, I know this is a criminal conspiracy I'm planning. I know right from wrong. The problem is I don't have anything else I can do, except to do the wrong thing in order to do the right thing. I can't go to the FBI. I really don't trust anyone over there, and they don't trust local prosecutors. If I go to them about their agent, he'll find out. Next thing I'll hear is how sad it is that the baby shows up dead or never found and there's no one on that boat. I get credit again for interfering in an FBI case, and that already happened once."

"I heard about that. I have to admit that I blamed you at first with that baby on the line. Then I heard the doctor and his nurse were murdered. Did the FBI agent do that?"

"Not sure, but he was in on it. May have even ordered it, but they knew too much, and I was on to them."

"I want to help, and I want in, but with my ass on the line, I need to know more about the plan and how solid this is. Fucking with the FBI isn't healthy, by the way, as you already know. I don't want to be the guy that takes the rap, if this deal of yours goes south."

"Even in a worst-case scenario, I don't think you will. The agent could never afford to talk about what we did, even if we can't get him to talk. The irony is, neither can we, but if we save the baby, we win."

"So, what's the plan?"

"Your part is to be on the back seat of a small six-seat airplane. You will be handcuffed with thick plastic ties like handcuffs, but the slide catches will be filed down so you can free yourself at any time, with little resistance. We will test that on the ground, and you might want to be the one who does the work and the testing. You will be wearing a winter overcoat, and a hood over your head. The hood will be fastened around your neck with a rubber band, and there will be a reason for that. We can't take the chance your hood gets blown off and you're recognized. Most importantly, you will only have a reserve parachute under your coat like the one you told me about last night. Lastly, there will be a cement block tied to your ankles that you can release with little effort, if it doesn't break free on its own. You will then simply wait, along with the pilot, until I show up with the agent who will also be tied up. Our part is a little more complicated."

"Do you actually have a pilot and a plane?"

"I do. He's a retired Marine colonel and works for a judge as his bailiff and pilot. We will be using the judge's plane on what the pilot calls a routine exercise flight. That's his only job in this, but he's in just as deep as the rest of us. He knows the risks and is willing to take them."

"So, what happens next? Sooner or later, it looks like I'm getting some airtime."

"Good guess," Spencer said smiling and remembering his conversation the night before about the terror of "airtime". "My job in this, with the help of my investigator, is to kidnap the agent and wrap him up. He will be hooded on his arrival at the plane, and his wrist ties will not be the detachable kind. His cement block won't be either. Once he's on the plane and we start the takeoff, I'll remove his hood and explain what he can do to save himself. If we're lucky, he'll crack, and it's over. If not, we'll go to an altitude you want, and I'll tell the agent the consequences of not talking. I'll tell him I have a suspect that has refused to talk. The agent won't believe me, and I'll mention the Florida guys to convince him that you are one of them. That should convince him, but if he still refuses to talk, I'll push you out. That's when I find out if the VC and the agent have anything in common. That's it."

"Remind me. Whether he talks or not, what are you planning to do with him?"

"Worst case, we let him go, and that's probably the end of it. There is no 'Plan B'. I have someone watching the boat, and I'm sure those four will simply disappear when they find out from the agent what happened to him and what I know. Between us, it's a Mexican standoff, with nothing more we can say or do. The same goes for the agent. Worst case, we never get the baby. Best case, we get the baby and still let him go. There's no way he goes anywhere with this, and the guys on his boat go free, too. I wish there was a way to fuck them up, but I don't see it."

"Who's going to help you kidnap that agent? All those agents carry guns and are well trained. You don't impress me as a strong-arm type. No offense."

"None taken. My investigator is the strong-arm type, and he can handle it. He's working up a plan as we speak to take him down."

"Is he ex-military, too?"

"No. He's ex-cop and a damn good one."

"How big is this FBI agent?" Walcott asked.

"From what I saw when I met him, he looks like a middle-aged banker with thinning hair in his middle fifties. I would say maybe five feet ten and not particularly overweight. He seemed a little stout, but that could have been his suit. All in all, I wouldn't say he's an athlete, and there's nothing out of the ordinary about him."

"I like the plan and my part in it. Considering what I saw in that ambulance, you wouldn't want me breaking him down. I might get carried away. I will need a climb up to 10,000 feet, just for insurance. It's a law of physics I learned about free fall, and that block won't cause me to come down any faster, if that's what you're thinking. Once I get my hands free, I can get rid of the hood and block before my chute opens. I'll have plenty of time for all that if the hood doesn't get blown off when you push me out."

"Like I said, that's the reason for the rubber band. When the door opens, it's going to be windy, and I don't want to take the chance he sees your face. I get the physics of free fall, but the reason for the block is twofold. First, I learned from the agent that he's afraid of heights and feels safer on water. Second, I'm going to tell him that I'm going to dump him, just like

I will you, over a river where his body will sink, and he will never be found. Of course, I'll tell him that he won't have to worry about drowning because the fall will kill him, and that he won't be going to McDonalds with us for lunch."

"You are one cold son-of-a-bitch," Walcott said, drawing out each word for emphasis.

"It's a lot easier when you're really not planning to kill anyone," Spencer reassured him. "If you're in, I will get everyone together tomorrow morning, if that works for you, and we can plan out the final details. What I would like you to do is work up your part, and I'll get those ties for you."

"Forget it. I have just the right ones, and since I really have the only ass on the line that might end up dead, I'll take care of everything I will need to make my end work right down to the cement block. I can do it all; just give me a call with a place and time. You know," Joe said considering what he just agreed to, "this is still my slow time of the year for farming, and I never dreamed I'd be into anything this crazy after finding that Simpson lady."

WEDNESDAY

6:30 P.M.

Chapter Twenty

Spencer and his team met at his apartment early the next day to go over final details and assignments. It was now day twelve after the assault and at the statistical length of hospitalization for the Simpson's baby, if that accounted for why the baby had not made it to Rollins' boat. Smith was a true organizer in military style, but not overbearing, and to him and Walcott, it was a military operation with one objective – save the baby.

After all the introductions and the establishment of a mutual comfort level with the plan in general, Smith began with a weather report for the next day, which was the first question that was on everyone's mind.

"I checked the weather, and it looks like good VFR. That means it will be good for what we're doing. No adverse weather conditions and I won't have to file any flight plan with the FAA. There's also an onboard device that identifies the plane in the air, but I can disable it for a short local flight without any significant problems, as long as we stay out of a control area. In that case, I would have to identify myself, but with a disabled transponder, the I.D. thing, I can give a bogus call sign for a short flight that doesn't match the airplane. With the easy stuff out of the way, how do you plan to get Rollins away from his office?" Smith asked Butler.

"I'm open to other ideas, but I think we can get him alone by Spencer calling him and saying that he got a call from an informant that wants to help and has some information about people in Florida. When he hears Florida, we'll have his undivided attention. Spencer then tells Rollins that the informant wants a meeting, but Spencer, in keeping with his promise not to interfere, asks Rollins to handle it and tells Rollins he will take him to the informant. Unless there's more than one agent involved, Rollins will meet Spencer alone. If he brings someone, just like Spencer will bring me, we'll have to scrub it or convince Rollins that four's a crowd. I'll make sure he takes the front passenger seat, and Spencer will pull into Alter Park not far from his office, but off the beaten path. When we get there, I'll loop a belt over his neck and pull hard, but not enough to hurt him or leave a mark. Spencer will immediately disarm him. I expect he will have two pistols. I expect he'll have a cell phone and we need to disable the GPS function by turning off the phone or by removing the battery. We can't let it track us to the airport. I do expect there will be a struggle, probably violent, and Spencer will have to get cuffs on him and stuff a rag in his mouth. His feet will have to be bound, too. Spencer, you will have to get him to the floor out of sight. Can't be driving up to a stop light with a hooded front seat passenger next to another car. I think that's the best we can do. Once the hood is on, we take him to the plane and load him in. The rest is up to Spencer and Walcott. Just for insurance, I'll have a recorder on, in case Rollins decides to do something stupid later after we get his confession."

"I'm hoping for a confession, but you have to know that while a recording might save us later, it's worthless for a criminal charge against Rollins. But I still say the recorder is a good idea," Spencer advised.

"I don't like the way you're going to get control of Rollins," Walcott said. "He might not be able to scream, but he will sure as hell be kicking and swinging. It'll be assholes and elbows. Even if you get one cuff on, that arm is now more dangerous than his fist with a swinging cuff. I think you know that. He'll probably kick out the front window, and Butler won't be able to help, other than to hold him back," Walcott said.

"I agree, but if I hit him in the head, I might kill him. I was thinking of using ether, but it would stink up the car so bad, he would smell it coming," Butler explained.

"I say we give him some of his own medicine," Spencer began. "I had a rape case not long ago. You may have heard about it. The rapist's M.O. was to give his victims a little shot of this narcotic that put girls under quickly for about fifteen minutes. There's nothing lethal about it, unless I overdo it.

179

I can get that stuff out of evidence in that case along with a couple of his left-over syringes. If I break one, I'll have a spare. Lesson learned from the Thomas case. I think the strap part will work because he should grab at his throat first, and when he does, I'll inject him right through his coat. It will be violent for a couple of minutes until he settles down, but after that, he's all ours."

"Good call, Spencer," Butler said, and there was agreement by Walcott and Smith.

"What time of day are you planning to pull this off?" Smith asked. "My reason for asking is that there's always someone around the airport as a home away from home and anxious to engage in hangar talk.

"We should be at the gate close to 4:30," Spencer volunteered.

"Those folks mean well," Smith continued, "but a real pain in the ass when you're trying to concentrate on the preflight exam of an airplane. What I'll want to do is get to the hangar early and do a preflight with the hangar door closed. Speaking of doors, I took off part of the rear door, so remember, it's going to be windy from the start of the takeoff to the landing. Don't worry. No one's going to get sucked out or blown out. That's only in the movies, but you still have to be careful, and Walcott's the only one with a chute. When you get close with Rollins, call me, and I'll open the hangar and check for visitors. If we do this after four in the afternoon, a lot of those guys are usually gone, but who knows? If the coast is clear, I'll meet you at the security gate and open it. You can then follow me to the hangar and pull in. I'll close the hangar door so we can load Rollins without being seen and get Joe situated looking his part. Any questions?"

"None so far," Spencer said. "Let's meet at the plane tomorrow morning and go over all the details one more time. I'll call Rollins from there, while we're all together so we will all know it's a go. Joe, do you have everything you need, like the ties and the cement block? We'll need another one for Rollins."

"It's all ready to go. I'll bring the block for Rollins. I'll be there with everything I need. All I want to do is sit back with my hood on, my reserve chute ready and wrist ties and cement
180

block attached. I'll probably take a nap until the engine starts. The rest is up to you guys. Remember, I need the plane to be at 10,000 feet before you throw me out."

"No problem there. I'll get you to 10,000 feet in about 20 minutes. That's figuring a normal climb at 500 feet per minute, and that should give you plenty of time to get to the point with Rollins," Smith said, looking at Spencer. "I am going to take a course along a river, so you should be able to point that out to Rollins anywhere along the route. If possible, I would like him facing backwards at all times so he can't identify the plane, or me, for that matter. But it is what it is, and I just don't want this to get back to the judge somehow."

"I'll try. I'll keep his attention toward me until I push Joe out," Spencer said.

"Getting a little nervous, are we, Colonel?" Walcott asked. He took a small measure of joy, that unlike him, his superior officer had mortal fears.

"Actually, yes. I think we all are or should be. This is a major crime against a major criminal, and frankly, he's all that's keeping me in this. It's a good thing we won't have our heads examined, and in the end, maybe we will. This guy Rollins deserves the needle in more ways than what Spencer is going to do, but I have to say I'm a little worried about him playing doctor with a drug he pilfered from one of his cases. If it kills him and we get caught, I think our only defense will be insanity!"

"In all the cases I have had where this stuff has been used, no one died, and I never heard it was lethal. If anyone wants out, now is the time to do it," Spencer stated, and no one answered. "Good. So, then we're on for tomorrow, and I hope we don't run out of time. Butler, I want you to make another call to Arnold, and considering the possibility the baby has been released from a hospital, tell him to be extra vigilant for the woman and baby showing up while we're putting this into action."

"Good thought and I'll take care of it," Butler answered, as Spencer continued.

"First thing in the morning, Spencer said, "we meet at the plane and get the security entrance and door thing worked out. Joe, you will stay at the hanger and wait for us. Colonel, you can expect Butler and me to arrive around 4:30 with Rollins. Tonight, I'll get the drug lined up, and Butler, I assume you have a belt or something you want initially to choke Rollins while I inject him, right?"

"Right, but I have a problem with you making your informant pitch to Rollins so early in the morning. Why not wait until shortly before we agree to pick him up? Why give him time to consider the reality of what's happening with an informant? Too early, and we lose the element of surprise," Butler said.

"I agree. Too much time and he'll figure it would be impossible to have an informant. I'll make the call around 3:15. If he's unavailable, well just call it off until I can reach him and reschedule. I would hate to see the wheels come off the wagon because Rollins is out for some reason, but anything at this point is possible. I guess that's it," Spencer said. "See you at the plane at 0700."

THURSDAY

8:00 A.M.

Chapter Twenty-One

The next morning, day thirteen after the assault, everyone met at Smith's hangar, and the final details were gone over again. It was a simple plan with few variables. Keeping it simple was a primary objective of all concerned, and each knew their assigned tasks. Spencer was the only one who kept track of the possible medical deadline they worked against. He felt a hint of superstition about unlucky number 13 and another law – Murphy's Law – that what can go wrong, will go wrong. They were already one day behind, but this was no time for doubts, he thought, and pushed superstition and worry aside.

Smith had already removed the plane's side entry door, and Walcott went through a dress rehearsal combining his overcoat with his hidden reserve chute, and his hand and leg ties that were rigged for an easy release. His main concern was making sure there would be enough daylight left to make the jump, and Smith assured him there would be, if everything went on schedule. Smith had the plane fueled, and it looked big and sleek even with just a single engine. Spencer had his syringes filled and ready with the knock-out juice, and Butler had an extra-long leather belt that he picked out at an all-night super store. He had also made the call to Arnold who reported no activity, except that he sold another painting to a tourist and got rid of the earring. Unfortunately for him, there were no rooms available while he kept watch, and his secret service detail and sun burn were beginning to wear on him. All that was left to do now was waiting until 3:15 P.M. to put in the call to Rollins.

Waiting was the hardest and most unexpected part of the plan. With everything done that had to be done, each member of the team was alone in their thoughts. Each one had unspoken and unresolved doubts about what, and why,

184

they had all come together to commit crimes that could put their futures on the line. For Spencer, it was classic approach/avoidance that he read about in a college psychology course. It was true, he thought. The closer he got to the objective, the more there was a push back to avoid it. If that is the force against it now, he thought, how strong would it be when he came face to face with Rollins? "Would I be the one to cut and run?" he questioned himself. "Would I be the one that the best men I could find would see me as the worst?" Not being seen now as a coward was more important to him than what the future may hold if the plan failed, and there was no turning back. The time had finally come to make the call.

"Is Agent Rollins in?" Spencer asked from his cell phone and was put through. "Hello, John. This is Spencer Tallbridge, and something has come up that I need to tell you about. I learned my lesson about screwing up your case."

"Are you talking about the Simpson case?" he asked.

"Sorry. Yes. I'm sure you have plenty of others. Well, I got this call from a woman who says she wants to talk to me today and claims to have information that might lead to the Simpson attackers. She said something about Florida, and she can hand them over, but wants protection. She also asked about any reward. I can handle the reward part, but this is your case, so I'm out, except for putting you together with her this afternoon. If you're not interested, I can meet her and fill you in later, if you think there's nothing to it."

"We don't know what we don't know, right? What time?"

"She just called and said 4:00 o'clock. I told her I'm bringing my two investigators, so she'll assume you're one of mine, okay?"

"Works for me. What time are you picking me up?"

"It's 3:20 and I'll be at your office in fifteen minutes. I'll call when I get close and meet you outside. Hopefully, it won't take too long. We ought to know quickly if she's the real deal or just a nut case."

Spencer was already in the neighborhood but parked to give the appearance of travel time before calling to let Rollins know he was close. Butler switched to the back seat, but for him, there was a problem.

"This doesn't look right. We pull up with me in the back seat, you in the front, and it looks like a set up. I need to be in the front seat, and I'll volunteer to give him the front seat when he meets us. That seems more normal to me."

"Where are you keeping the belt?" Spencer asked.

"Under the front passenger seat."

At close to 3:30 P.M., Spencer called to let Rollins know they were only minutes to arrival, and Rollins was already out and waiting. Spencer pulled up, and Rollins immediately opened the back passenger door as Butler got out and offered him the front seat.

"Agent Rollins, I'm Jake Butler, one of Spencer's investigators. Please take the front seat."

"Not a chance. This is your show, and I'm just along for the ride. Besides, I think there's a little more leg room back here." As he settled in, he asked, "You lose a belt, Spencer? Looks like there's a new one under the seat with a label on it."

"Damn, I wondered what happened to that. I just bought that and thought I lost it," Spencer said disarmingly.

"Tell me. Where's this meeting supposed to take place?"

"She said Alter Park, and she said she was very concerned that someone might see her talking to us. We'll have to play it by ear. Right, Butler?" Spencer asked, giving a coded message that he hoped Butler would understand that the plan was still on, but would be improvised.

When they arrived at Alter Park, it was entirely empty. There were no parked cars, and no one was seen walking through. No doubt, the cold weather played a role in that, as well as the time that was just a couple of hours before sunset.

"I think we're early, and she should be happy with no one here but us," Spencer said. "Let's go over to that picnic table where she can see us."

All three got out of Spencer's car, and Spencer quickly walked around to the door that Rollins would use. As Rollins began to step out, Spencer directed Rollins' attention to an imaginary someone he said might be the informant. As Rollins looked in that direction, Spencer punched him one time in the center of his chest as hard as he could, and in an area known as the solar plexus. Spencer knew enough from all his discussions with police officers that a hit there should paralyze anyone momentarily, and it worked. Rollins was stunned, speechless and dropped to his knees. Essentially, the wind was knocked out of him, but he recovered quickly and still had to be restrained before the effect of the punch wore off. Butler immediately took over and used the ties handed to him by Spencer, and also frisked him for weapons. Two pistols were found as expected. One was strapped to his left ankle, and the other was under his left shoulder. Butler looked them over and unloaded both while Spencer continued to search and found Rollins' cell phone that was already turned off. Rollins was just as quickly gagged, hooded, pushed to the floor of the front passenger seat and was now ready for transport.

"Didn't know you had a 'Plan B' in you, Spencer. Good job," Butler said. "I'll make the call and let them know we're on our way."

"Thanks. I was worried about the needle trick anyway. Funny how things work out. Fortunately, I didn't end up with a one-punch homicide," Spencer said, thinking of the few times that a simple street fight ended with one ill-fated punch that killed someone, and the percentages in his favor against such a result. Usually, the fatalities came from a single strike to the head or a fall back ending with a fatal basal skull fracture.

Now, it was game on. Spencer had crossed the line between the abstract and reality. He knew there was no turning back. In an instant, he perceived that his whole world had changed. There was no longer a sense of shared responsibility. It was all on him, he thought, and those who considered themselves his partners in crime were merely the instruments of the enterprise he had cobbled together. Shared or not, they were all losing the light, and no time could be wasted for further reflection. Completing the mission was all that mattered, and no more words were spoken between Spencer and Butler during the drive to the plane except the call to Smith that they were on their way.

Chapter Twenty-Two

On the drive to the hangar, Rollins struggled non-stop against his restraints. His groans and grunts under his hood, signaled he would have plenty to say when the gag and hood were removed. At the airport, Smith was waiting at the security entrance and flagged them in. Other than the means of kidnapping Rollins, the plan was falling in place. When they arrived at the hangar, Smith said that no one was making the rounds for hangar talk. "Good thing," Smith said, because he wasn't sure how he would explain taking the rear door off the judge's airplane.

There was just enough room for Spencer to drive into the hangar, and once done, Smith closed the door so that Rollins could be unloaded without the risk of being seen. He continued to struggle, but he was wearing down. With the plane door removed, Smith directed Spencer and Butler to headsets for their use and another for Rollins. The recorder was also plugged into the system to make a recording of anything Rollins might say after his hood was removed and his headset was in place. Walcott was already seated wearing his hood and his bulky overcoat to hide his reserve parachute. The cement block stood out prominently attached to his leg to eventually catch Rollins' eyes. When Spencer arrived with Butler and Rollins, Walcott began to twist slowly against his apparent restraints and mumble something indistinguishable, as planned for the benefit of Rollins.

Butler took great care to make the final tie down of Rollins in the plane, including attaching a cement block to his left leg. All of their lives would be in danger if he got loose. Once everything was done that had to be done on the ground, Smith told Spencer to open the hangar door, and Smith used a small gas-powered tow to pull out the plane. Once out, Spencer and Butler took their assigned seats with Spencer sitting next to

Walcott who was next to the open door. Walcott already had a seat belt in place, and Spencer strapped himself in. Butler sat next to Rollins, who had also been strapped in, and both of them faced Spencer and Walcott. The last one in was Smith, who took the left front pilot seat and called out, "Clear Prop!" before starting the engine. That was a standard pilot warning that a propeller would be on the move and might not be seen by the unwary. Rollins became more animated in his struggles against his restraints as the plane taxied to the runway for takeoff, and although Spencer was anxious to confront Rollins, no action would be taken, or his hood removed until they were airborne.

The takeoff was noisy and windy, but uneventful, as Smith slowly climbed the plane toward the designated altitude and destination along a river below. It was finally time for the main event. Spencer signaled Butler to remove Rollins' hood and remove the rag in his mouth. Removing those triggered his anticipated reaction.

"What the fuck is going on, you assholes? You've kidnapped and assaulted a federal officer, and you're all under arrest," Rollins shouted, but no one could hear him over the wind howling through the cabin. Butler immediately put a headset on Rollins, and he repeated his statement exactly as first given. No one replied.

"What the hell is going on?" Rollins again questioned. "My office knows I'm with you. You're going down for this."

"Don't believe him Spencer," Butler said. "He never told his office anything about us, but I think he had his own plan if we had an informant. One of his guns is a Charter Armament revolver, a throwaway, with the serial numbers ground down. It would probably be found at the park with a dead you, me, and if we had one, our informant."

"That explains why his phone was off when I picked his pocket," Spencer confirmed.

Rollins started to respond, and Spencer interrupted abruptly, "Shut the fuck up. Colonel, can you make a phone call from here?"

"I can if I keep us below 2,000. What do you need?"

"I want you to call Rollins' office. I have the number. Tell his secretary you are me and looking for Rollins. Just find out what she says."

With that and the number, Smith made the call and reported. "She said he's at his doctor's office and won't be back for a couple of hours. I'm continuing the climb to 10,000."

"It doesn't make any difference. You're all finished," Rollins said confidently.

"I don't think you're in any position to be making threats, Rollins," Spencer said. "We know your involvement in the Simpson case. We know all about your crew in Florida on your boat, and we just can't get this guy to tell us where the baby is. That's where you come in. You have a chance for a soft landing or a hard one, but I think you're going to tell us."

"You're crazy. I'm not a criminal. You're making a big mistake. You better think this through while you still can."

"We already have, and you have been found guilty as charged. It's just the finish now. You're in it for the money. We know that. You're rounding out your retirement. We know that, too. You're a rogue agent, and you can live or die with that. Tell us the truth now and you save yourself. We get the baby. That's all we want. I know I can't use your confession, and you get to move on. No one ever says anything about you, and vice versa. If you don't talk, out you go to the bottom of a river two miles down," Spencer said pointing through the open door.

"You're bullshit. You're no killer. None of you are, and you're all going to prison for this. So you all found me guilty, and I'm supposed to get the death penalty. I heard about you. I know you're against it."

"I agree, but this isn't about justice, or even punishment," Spencer answered. "It's about war, and this is war, not a debate, and not really a jury trial. It's a no-holds-barred war and death is the final option of this tribunal, you miserable fuck."

"Bullshit, but who is that guy anyway?" Rollins said laughing now and looking at the hooded figure in front of him.

"He's one of yours. Pretty stubborn guy. He'd rather be in Florida on your boat, but wants to see Allah instead of
190

talking, and we're glad to accommodate. How much further?" Spencer called out to Smith.

"Just a little longer. Get ready. I'll let you know."

"You can save your guy, Rollins. What's it going to be?"

"Fuck you and the horse you rode in on, you little piss ant," Rollins said with more confidence that it was all a hoax. With that, Spencer picked up the cement block attached to Walcott, held it for a moment to give Rollins a chance to process what was happening and dropped it out the door with Walcott in tow.

"One down," Spencer said to Rollins. "From one little piss ant to one big son-of-a-bitch, this is your last chance, and frankly, I'm looking forward to you not taking it. You've disgraced the FBI, and I can live with this. You're up next. You will have about a minute on your way down to wish you talked before you hit the river. Let's get this over with."

With his voice now shaking and his whole body now trembling, Rollins forced out the words, "How do I know you won't kill me, too?" now confident it was no hoax.

"It all depends. Tell the truth, and I'll let you live. Lie to me, and then out you go. Make up your mind. We don't have much time before we lose the river."

"I didn't have anything to do with the Thomas killing or his nurse, and I didn't know they would try to kill Mrs. Simpson. I was against it. It was unnecessary, but in the end, they thought she saw too much even with their masks on. They decided to kill her, not me. You have to believe that, even if you think I would have killed you at the park. The baby got sick. It was a lung problem, and he's in a hospital. It's Rutledge where Mrs. Simpson was taken. The nurse actually got a job there as a part of this just in case there was a problem. With her in that position, they could hide the baby in plain sight. It really was the perfect plan. We even knew that someone was making the rounds asking questions about a baby being brought in, but we covered it with her. Last I heard, she may be taking the baby to Florida at any time because the baby is doing much better. I should get a call, though, because I'm their boat ride south out of the Keys."

"Who's doing this and why?" Butler asked.

"It's all about genetics as far as they're concerned. The attackers want the Simpson genes. They called it gene editing, and they think this is their best shot to build their genius gene pool."

"You mean you sold out your country for this?" Butler asked.

"No. It's a crazy plan. There is no valid science to it. I checked that out. There's just one of their crazy scientists who believes it and the rest have the money to try to make it work. Anyway, I get paid when they leave on my boat with the kid and not before. They don't know it, but I have insurance on that. They will kill me, if they find out I talked."

"You know I would've killed you if you didn't. How much and how many Americans are involved?" Spencer asked.

"Ten million dollars cash and no one else is involved at least not anymore after the doctor and nurse were murdered. The money's all in cash. It's a whole ice chest full to the lid. This is their first operation, but the same crew will be involved in more. They are a patient bunch. Waiting twenty years for breeding stock to develop is nothing to them, they tell me. It was so simple. I guess that's how you figured it out."

"Right. Even a country hick like me could figure it out. You arrogant asshole," Spencer said disparagingly. "Here's the program, Rollins. We're going to hold you at the airport until we get the baby. If everything pans out, I'll cut you lose. If you're lying, you're going to get one last flight the hard way, so you better hope we're in time at the hospital. Colonel, get us back ASAP, and if you can, notify Mr. and Mrs. Simpson to meet us at the Rutledge County Hospital. No matter what, I want her there, even if she is in a wheelchair," Spencer said.

"I've seen a lot of homicides, but I have never heard of a prosecutor killing a suspect, especially like this," Rollins said.

"Me neither," Spencer said, "and I'd rather not make it a twofer."

During the remainder of the flight back, nothing more was said. As they taxied to the hangar, Smith's cell phone went off. After a brief conversation, he turned back to Spencer to give him a thumbs up that Walcott was on the ground and in one piece. "So far, so good," Spencer thought to himself.

***

Spencer and Butler left Smith and Rollins with the plane and raced toward Rutledge Hospital breaking all speed limits. It wasn't long before a sheriff's cruiser came up from behind with its flashers on, and Spencer had a rare opportunity to flash his badge and handle it quickly.

"Official business, officer," Spencer said with commanding justification through his open window. "I am the Rutledge County Prosecutor, and I'd appreciate a high-speed escort to Rutledge Hospital."

"Yes, sir. Sorry I didn't recognize you. Just follow me. I'll slow down through red lights, so be prepared. I'll have to call it in. Can you tell me what this is all about?"

"I will, but not now. Let's get going."

When they arrived at the hospital, Spencer told the officer to tell the sheriff that he was at the hospital following up an emergency lead on the Simpson case. Just inside the main entrance doors, the Simpsons were both waiting with questioning expressions of why they were summoned to the hospital. As expected, Alice Simpson was not yet ambulatory and was guided by Carl in her wheelchair.

"Is this about our baby?" Carl asked.

"It is, and we have reason to believe your baby is here in the neonatal unit. We'll start there, and I'll explain later. Mrs. Simpson, I want you to try hard to remember the voice of the woman who was with those who assaulted you. She may be here and if you recognize her voice, you may remember more than what you've told. This is the time to remember, okay?"

"I'll try," she said.

Spencer left the officer behind to call in his report, and he, Butler and the Simpsons made their way to the main information desk to get directions to the neonatal unit. When they arrived at the neonatal unit, they were met by the charge nurse who was at a desk facing a large glass window where the entire unit was visible with several rows of filled baby cribs. Several nurses were seen attending the babies, and none seemed distracted by the four visitors now looking into the unit.

"Can I help you?" the charge nurse asked.

Spencer began to answer when Alice Simpson was seen grasping her husband's arm and urgently telling him something that Spencer could not hear.

"Is there a problem?" Spencer asked Carl.

"No. She just said she heard our baby. With all the babies crying in there, I guess it's natural. She'll be okay, but what now?"

Without answering, Spencer turned back to the charge nurse with his prosecutor badge in hand in full display and made his introduction.

"I'm Spencer Tallbridge, the Rutledge County Prosecutor', he said flashing his ID. This fellow is my chief investigator, and these folks are Mr. and Mrs. Simpson. You may have heard about them, and I have reason to believe their kidnapped baby is in your unit right now. I'm here to find out."

"I have to call my supervisor. You do understand that," she said.

"No. Actually, I don't. I'm looking for one of your nurses, and she's of Middle Eastern descent. Do you know who that may be?"

"I'm sorry, sir. I have to call my supervisor," she said as she picked up her desk phone.

Spencer quickly put his hand on hers and ordered her to stop. "This is a police matter, and stay out of our way unless you plan to help. Now, one more time, do you have a nurse with a foreign accent?" Spencer asked with all the authority he could muster.

"We do, and more than one. There is a new hire with an accent, and she is excellent. Neonatal nurses are hard to find. I can't imagine she's in any trouble. She was here a second ago. I saw her when you all came in. I just saw her leaving the floor with a baby that was crying and probably going for testing. I'm not sure. That goes on a lot here."

"How did she get past us?"

"She didn't have to. There's a doorway to the testing areas back there, and then an emergency exit. If you let me, I

194

can call for her."

"Jesus Christ," Spencer said. "She's on the run." Spencer grabbed the entrance door handle to the unit, but it was locked for security. "Open this door, or I'll knock it down," Spencer commanded instantly, and the nurse unhesitatingly pushed a button to let him in. Together, Spencer and Butler were now also on the run, and leaving the Simpsons behind. "We need to split up and head for any exits," Butler yelled. "We can lock down the hospital, but if she's headed out, we'll lose her for sure."

Spencer took the first emergency exit he saw to a stairway and lost sight of Butler, who continued down a corridor with numerous examination rooms and exit signs. Spencer heard a baby crying down the stairs he was taking and then the crashing sound of an exterior door. "Has to be her," he thought and shouted back to Butler to follow and hoping he heard his call. When he reached the bottom, he saw a nurse running across a parking lot with what appeared to be a bundled-up baby, and there was no way to stop her. She was too far away. Spencer called out for her to stop. She continued with not so much as a pause. Spencer continued running toward her at full speed, but she was 200 feet away when she reached a car, jerked open the rear passenger door and unceremoniously threw in the baby. She then got into the driver's seat and smiled at Spencer with her window down as she was about to start her car. At that moment, when Spencer was convinced that he had lost the foot race, a single gunshot rang out with a bullet hitting the nurse squarely in her forehead with lethal effect. It was Butler, who heard Spencer's call, and was able to close enough distance to take one good shot to end it.

Hospital security converged in all directions. Butler put both arms in the air and held his badge high. Spencer followed suit as both men were approached by security guards with their guns drawn and ready to fire.

"Don't shoot. We're law enforcement," Butler called out three times to make sure he was heard and understood. "There's a baby in that car, and I need to get it. That nurse is probably dead, and she's wanted for murder and kidnapping."

"I need I.D.," another guard ordered and it was given by Spencer, who also identified Butler as his investigator, with lawful authority to do what had been done. Soon, the air was filled with the sounds of sirens, and Carl could be seen pushing Alice in her wheelchair forward through the crowd that was forming.

"Let them through," Spencer yelled to a guard and pointing at Alice and Carl. There could now be heard a baby crying from the car with the dead nurse at the wheel. Carl pushed Alice to the car, and he reached into the back seat and carefully lifted the baby out into the waiting arms of Alice, now crying uncontrollably. Carl's tears were also flowing freely, and considering the McBride case, it was the second time in less than a year that Spencer had another emotional letdown. His tears also were flowing freely.

By this time, the Rutledge County Sheriff had arrived and took charge of the scene.

"Have a little dust in your eyes, do you? You want to tell me what the hell just happened?" he asked Spencer and gave further orders not to touch the pistol that Butler had carefully placed on the ground.

"Is that yours?" the sheriff asked Butler.

"It is. I shot her. She's one of the baby's kidnappers, and I didn't have a choice."

"Hell of a shot. I'll have to hang on to your weapon for a while, but you knew that. How did you put all this together?"

"An anonymous tip. We were told it was a Middle Eastern nurse that had the baby and that the baby was hidden in plain sight with a medical problem. It's a long story, but that's essentially it. When I saw her throw the baby in the car, I knew it was her, and I had to take the shot even at about 50 yards. Really more luck than accuracy, and she was just about on the move. No innocent nurse or mother would have done what I saw her do with the baby just as I was catching up with Spencer," Butler said, as Spencer listened nearby to the story he told.

"Here all the time. Who would have thought it? You know we still have to do DNA on the baby. God help you both, if you're wrong on this. Never had anything like this before.

196

What do I do with the baby now?" the sheriff asked.

"Good luck in trying to take that baby from the Simpsons, but I know they will cooperate with any testing," Spencer said. "I really want them to put the baby back in the hospital unit until it's medically cleared. You can do any testing while that's going on."

Butler then continued to talk with the sheriff about the chase, and Spencer walked off a short distance to make a call back to Smith.

"Hello, Colonel. Let Joe know that it's over and over in a big way. We found the nurse and the baby, and Butler shot her in the head. The Simpsons have the baby now, and we can cut Rollins lose. Let me talk to him."

Without any questions about what happened, Smith held the phone to the ear of the still shackled Rollins, who was held in the back of the plane.

"It's over, Rollins. The nurse is dead, and the baby is back with the Simpsons. The sheriff was told we got an anonymous tip, so you and I have a Mexican standoff. We're far from even, but there's nothing either one of us can do about that."

"How are you going to explain the guy you murdered today? That's not on me."

"Gotcha, you prick. Payback is a bitch. No one got murdered today. That was an American hero, who was rigged up with a reserve chute and slip ties on his wrists. The cement block is at the bottom of the river. He's fine. You fell for it harder than you would have landed, if I couldn't convince you to talk. I guess we will never know what I would have done with you if you didn't. Anyway, we have a Mexican standoff. I can't use your confession, and you can't charge us. I think early retirement for you is a real good idea. The guys on your boat are your problem. If they figure this out, I agree with you that they'll kill you – not that you don't deserve it."

"I told you I have insurance. I expect when they hear about this they will leave without me, and I expect them to leave permanently. How in hell did you figure this all out? How did you come up with the guys in Florida?"

"For you, that's the hell of it. You don't get to know. What you do need to know is that a tape recorder was plugged into your headset, so I've got insurance, too. Just so you know. Put the pilot back on."

"What now, Spencer?" Smith asked.

"Cut him loose. He won't cause us any trouble. Give him back his weapons, unloaded, and his cell phone. Give him a ride, if you want to, but tell him nothing. The media is here now along with the sheriff. This is going to be a big news event nationwide in about five minutes, and I have to get back to the Simpsons."

Chapter Twenty-Three

The Simpsons were with the sheriff, and Alice was cradling her baby when Spencer approached them. The sheriff had already told them about the need for DNA testing, although they were confident that the baby was theirs. Alice was the first to greet Spencer.

"How can we ever thank you, Mr. Tallbridge?"

"You can't," Spencer said with a smile. "I'm just glad it's over. There were a lot more ways this could have gone wrong than right. I think luck played a big role, and maybe a small miracle or two."

"How about that Spencer's Law?" the sheriff asked in good humor. "Did it play a part?"

"What's that? What's Spencer's Law?" Alice asked.

"It's just something I consider in tough cases. Wait long enough and good things will happen. You just have to keep faith that the good things will be on your side and not the other," Spencer explained.

"Do you think this is over? Are we still in any danger? What about the others that did this to us?" Carl asked.

"I can't say it's over, and there may still be danger. The tip I received indicates that a rogue group in a foreign country is behind this and wanted your baby because of Carl's genius," Spencer said looking down at Alice. "It's the selective breeding thing to achieve modernity. I know the sheriff will take care of your security now."

"Can I put that out now? I mean about your tip and the foreign country?" the sheriff asked.

"Absolutely. I think it will help to put a stop to this, at least as far as the Simpsons are concerned."

"I'll get a press release out on that. Do you want to call the feds or should I?" the sheriff asked.

"You do it, and tell Rollins I said hello. Alice, I do have one question. I brought you here today because I thought you may be able to recognize the voice of the woman who was involved in all this. You never heard her voice today, but you said you heard your baby crying. How did you know it was your baby?"

"I know I wanted any crying baby to be mine, and there were so many, but I have to tell you there was something deep inside that said that one baby I heard was mine when we first walked up to the unit. I knew it. I was positive. That's all I can tell you."

"I think there's more to penguins than we know," Spencer said cryptically without further explanation. That would come another day with his friend Janet at Dog by the Pound. About an hour after the news alert hit the airwaves, Arnold called Spencer with a report and excitement in his voice.

"Something's going on, Boss. I think they're on the move."

"What makes you thinks so?"

"One of the guys left the boat about ten minutes ago and the other three are all pacing around and looking at their cell phones. I don't know if they're waiting for that fourth guy, but something's up. Still, no woman and no baby. Wait a minute. The fourth guy is walking up fast on the pier, and the others are untying the mooring lines. I think they're leaving. Do you want me to contact the sheriff down here now?"

"No, just let 'em go."

"The engine just started up, and the boat is backing out. It's starting to turn and..."

Suddenly, there was the deafening sound of an explosion, and Arnold started yelling.

"Holy shit! Did you hear that?" he exclaimed. "That was the boat blowing up! Pieces are flying everywhere. There's a huge fire ball! Those guys have to be dead. No one could survive that. The boat's gone! I mean gone! What's going on?" Arnold asked.

"Come on home, Arnold. We'll talk about it when you get back. Right now, I've two calls to make: one to a very wise old man, and the other to a beautiful young lady – my Irish lucky charm. As far as those guys are concerned, sounds like the devil just collected on a rigged up insurance policy. Case closed."

The End

About the Author

Michael T. Gmoser is the Prosecuting Attorney of Butler County, Ohio, who started out as a trial attorney and then worked his way through the legal system. He has received awards for excellence along with recognition that his ethics and trial skills are "preeminent" with a Martindale-Hubbell rating of AV, the highest possible from that nationally recognized attorney rating service.

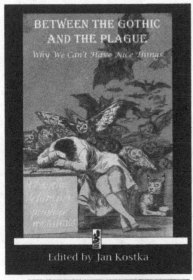
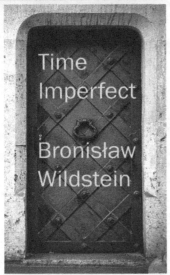